For Evan; LeanNE

I inniatted your name
on the "acknowledgements
page"

Enjoyed our visit last
spring
Hope to get a hike in
again sometime soon

Love
Auntie Laverne

FIREWEED

LAVERYNE GREEN

FIREWEED

iUniverse books may be ordered through booksellers or by contacting:

iUniverse
1663 Liberty Drive
Bloomington, IN 47403
www.iuniverse.com
1-800-Authors (1-800-288-4677)

ISBN: 978-1-6632-0477-6 (sc)
ISBN: 978-1-6632-0478-3 (e)

Library of Congress Control Number: 2020912239

Print information available on the last page.

iUniverse rev. date: 07/21/2020

This story is dedicated to those who have experienced a loss through the death of a core loved one, particularly when in their formative years.

ACKNOWLEDGEMENTS

A belated thank-you to my niece, Leanne Smailes, who phoned one night and predicted I'd write a book. It felt like a terrifying life sentence at the time, but I have enjoyed the journey.

Thank you to my long-time friend Linda Timmermans, who applauded my phraseology over the years and always said I should write a book.

I give soulful thanks to the many friends and clients who, over multiple years, shared their unique experiences and perspectives of their grief journey and added insight to this writing.

I am grateful for the warm welcome and extended hospitality shown by Jeff and Jodi Snyder while I toured and researched Germany for part of this story.

Thanks to my Tigger friend, Kelly Berg, for her eternal use of speaking in parables that delve deep and ferret out real meaning in situations. Our many times spent sharing a cup of tea in front of her fireplace, discussing life in general while reviewing the fledgling manuscript, will be cherished memories for me when I think of this book.

Thank you to Eleanor Russell, whom I trusted to be my first reader of this story and who gave helpful, constructive criticism.

To Sheila Baumbach, with the Canadian Mental Health Association, for sharing her wise and caring heart and her resourceful assistance, and for opening up opportunities for me to interface with a multitude of grieving folks from teens to the elderly—thank you so much.

Special gratitude to Dallas Reimer, Lesley Unruh, and Jodi Snyder, three sisters who inspired the theme of this story. I hope you recognize a few similarities to your story.

Finally, a big thank you to Bradley for his generous spirit, which has given me freedom to cloister myself away and work on this book.

PROLOGUE

Summer 1984

The nasty alarm, my night-shift archenemy, blares me awake. I deftly silence it without really looking, and I know my precious sleep time is over. It was a brutal twelve-hour shift last night. I loathe night shifts; I'm sure each one robs me of at least three days' life expectancy!

Living in Macklin, Saskatchewan, but working in small-town Provost, Alberta, plus having differing time zones, creates barriers; both add to the mix.

Attempting to open my scratchy, sleep-deprived eyes, I appreciate the gentle rosy glow awash in the room. Heavy aubergine drapery covers the large French doors to our second-floor bedroom deck but allows some summer sun to filter through, and I allow myself to luxuriate a little longer in the big king-size brass bed.

A second peek at the clock reveals it is almost noon, meaning my girls will soon be rushing in the back door, coming home from the neighbour's house.

How thankful I am that my hubby, Quinn, was home to care for the girls last night and get them off safely to the sitter this morning

I sit on the edge of the bed waiting for my head to clear and find myself studying our recent family photo gracing the wall in front of me. Provost Photography has done an amazing job, capturing our moment in time. It seems like Quinn's blue eyes look directly at me with the ever-present, fun-loving twinkle, and I hear his ready laugh in my mind. He's not smiling, though; he believes an official picture should be serious. I chuckle, remembering him being assigned the sitting position because he's a full foot taller than me. I stand proudly behind him with one hand on his broad shoulder and my long, dark hair framing my oval face. I'm smiling and looking down at six-year-old Gina, who is tall for her age and fair, with sun-sensitive skin and blue eyes, like her dad. I remember nearly laughing, not just smiling, as I looked at her in her new, unplanned, little-boy haircut she had managed all by herself just the day before our sitting. We couldn't wait for it to grow out; it wasn't easy to get a sitting with this photographer.

Eight-year-old Noelle-Cheri, with dark curls, looking the most like me, is posed to look at her dad. But I can discern mischief in her stance and those hazel eyes; she didn't want to waste time doing a photo shoot, I recall. She stands as instructed though, with one arm draped casually around her ten-year-old sister, Victoria. Quinn has dubbed her our "blue-eyed china doll." Her curl-resistant long blonde hair, big blue eyes, and wide smile atop a slim frame and stick legs were somehow the inspiration for the moniker that has stuck through the years.

My heart feels so bubbly full as I study the picture, and I acknowledge afresh that I love my professional life as a nurse, but I get my real sense of worth from Quinn's love and together parenting these three rascals.

I finally jump up and wrap myself in a cheery striped cotton robe and head to the bathroom. I sit on the edge of the tub and press a warm cloth to my tired face and eyes—my favourite waking ritual. A quick application of facial moisturizer and a scrunchie to twist up my curls, and I'm done with my elaborate primping for now.

A gate latch closing and feet running on the back deck indicate the girls' arrival.

It's laughable to think I didn't even want kids when we got married. But as a few years passed, I reconsidered my view and decided one child might be manageable.

Then two more came along—a little too quickly and definitely unplanned.

I think I've learned it's sometimes beneficial to have some unplanned things happen in life just as a reminder we are not totally in control of things.

I hear a lively discussion taking place as they pause at the back door, and I'm not surprised they are focused on one of those very unplanned, no-control-over events of just two days ago.

"What's a eulogy?" I hear Gina ask her older sisters.

"I think it's telling about the one who's died," I hear Victoria reply cautiously.

"I'm going to do the eulogy," Noelle-Cheri pipes in fervently. Surprisingly, I don't hear any argument from the other two.

"Torr, I think you should be the pastor and do the prayers," Gina adds.

"But what will you do, Gina?" comes the chorused request from the older two in unison.

"I want to place a wreath. I'll lay it against the bird feeder. I've already started making it. Dad found me some wire last night and helped me cut some branches from that tree; it's the one she liked to climb most often."

"Yeah, and Dad had to help her get back down often too!" I hear Torr remind.

"Can we help, Gina? We could add flowers from the garden?" both sisters ask.

I'm not surprised at their discussion. I know their grief is raw. Our family feline, Josephine, met her ninth life just two days ago. A truck driver left her rather flattened and definitely, irrevocably, dead.

We all had taken a turn digging the deep, deep grave in the northeast corner of our thriving garden, under the heavy bird feeder, between the lush purple fireweed and the tall, showy sunflowers. Gina chose the location, and for once the vote was unanimous.

Our funeral for Josephine is planned for tomorrow, Saturday. The burial had to be immediate because of the hot weather, but I had begged for a delay in the funeral. "So Dad and I can both be present," I had reasoned.

I marvel at their different reactions to their loss of Josephine. Sensitive Victoria cried a lot and accepted my hugs and sympathy. Mysterious Noelle-Cheri seemed angry and spent as much time away with her friends as allowed. Industrious Gina got busy scouring for as many photos of Josephine as she could find and plastered them mostly on the walls in her room, but I've noticed a few placed around the house too. I suspect I will find more today.

I hope our family feline funeral tomorrow is helpful for them. I feel inadequate being a grief counsellor.

BOOK 1

Noelle-Cheri (N. C.)

28 December 1989

This is a very important day; I'm too excited to sleep in even though it's the middle of Christmas holidays! Lucky for me, Dad needed to be back at work today, so we're all back home from visiting family and friends. Most importantly, I'm back in time for Tosh's sleepover birthday party! She and I have been planning it ever since my birthday party, which was exactly two months ago. So today we're both thirteen, and we call ourselves twins just two months apart. We're definitely not identical twins. Tosh is a fair bit taller, has steel-grey eyes, and wears her heavy blonde hair in a spiky cut, while I have a compact, petite build; wear my dark hair in loose curls down to my shoulder blades; and have eyes of a greenish colour. We think alike, though, and we create chaos whenever and wherever we can.

Since Dad transferred to Fort McMurray three years ago, Tosh has become my best friend. This city, spread throughout the river valleys, makes us feel as though we are living in the mountains, and we ended up in Beacon Hill, just a few doors down from Tosh. We go to the same school and love our principal, Ms Potter, who enjoys our kind of creativity, and we joined the city junior drama team together. I'm also taking piano lessons (boring) and figure skating (sort of fun), and now I'm old enough to go to "youth" at church too.

Today seems to be dragging, even though Mom seems to have a lot of assignments for me. Grandma and Grandpa came back with us from Red Deer and are staying over New Year's. Lots of family are also braving the long trek to Fort McMurray to ring in the new year with us. It's going to be a busy few days, but it should be fun too. However, it looks like I am child labour at my mom's disposal. I frown and think, *It doesn't look like Torr or Gina are being kept as busy.*

Hearing the phone, I race to the kitchen to get it before my siblings. I'm sure it's Tosh, and we have so much to discuss. I nearly collide with Mom, who is ironing Dad's jeans in the front hallway.

"Sorry, Mom," I throw back at her as I whizz by.

"Slow down, speedy; you might run over Grandma or Grandpa, you know," she cautions.

"Hello," I answer the phone breathlessly, and quickly head to the laundry room for privacy, dragging our three-mile cord behind me. "Tosh?"

"It's me all right. When did you get back? Do you have all the stuff packed for tonight?"

"Definitely. You know me. Made my list and checked it twice! I've got the ghetto blaster, sleeping bag and pillow, make-up galore, Nerd and Skittles stash, and my Miss Hannigan props." I then burst out singing: "Some women are dripping with diamonds. Some women are dripping with pearls. Lucky me. Lucky me. Look at what I'm dripping with ... Little girls!"

"You do such a great job of her, N. C. I can't wait to get back to rehearsals next week. Hey, why not bring your *Cats* costume from last year's play too. Doing that make-up is so totally tubular!" suggested Tosh.

"Great plan. I should be able to find it. We can do up all the other girls as cats too. Love your crazy ideas, Tosh."

"Crazy. I was crazy once," she starts.

"They put me in a rubber room," I say, continuing the circular mantra.

"It was full of rats. I hate rats!"

"They drive me crazy."

"Crazy. I was crazy once ..."

Our bantering usually ends with this or a word challenge. We both have this fascination with interesting words.

"Hey, how are you getting over here with all that stuff tonight, N. C.?"

"Mom will be busy here, but Dad will be home from work by then, and he'll drop me off with all the extras. Don't worry about me."

"Bus is leaving in five!" I hear Mom call.

"Happy thirteenth birthday Tosh—*twin* Tosh! I gotta

run—heading to the mall, and the bus is leaving tout de suite, so au revoir, Tosh," I say and quickly hang up.

As I see Gina, Miss "Ready Freddie," and her bosom buddy, Maggie, dart out the door, I notice Torr at the dining room table, looking studious, head down, her wavy amber hair hiding her face and lazy Borneo curled up on her lap.

"Did you hear Mom call?"

Without looking up from her books, she answers, "Yes, but I'm staying home to start on this homework assignment. If I want to stay on the honour roll, I need to get this ready to hand in our first day back."

"Then see you later, alligator. I'm not missing a chance to get to the mall. Maybe I'll bring back some black liquorice for you to share with Dad." *I don't know how they can eat that horrid stuff*, I think with a shudder as I grab my parka but neglect to slip on winter boots.

Our deep-freeze, deep-snow winter has not let up, and as we back out of the garage and down our steep driveway, all six of us hang on as Mom accelerates with a roar of the trusty van engine to plough through the accumulated bank, where our nicely shovelled portion meets the street. And we're off. Peter Pond Mall, here I come!

Barf me out! Mom's stopping at the grocery store first. It's right beside the mall, but I haven't dressed for even a short walk in this minus-thirty winter freeze. I guess I'll just help her make some *good* food choices and be patient—not my nature.

The grocery cart looks full and overflowing. I'm hopeful we'll all head to the real stores now. I need a special card for Tosh too.

"Girls, help me find Grandma and Grandpa. We need to head home right now," Mom states firmly as her eyes dart every which way and she bites on her lower lip.

"Mom, what's the matter; are you sick?" Gina asks, sounding worried. "We need to go through checkout first."

"No. We need to go home right now. I don't know why" is the strange answer.

We find Grandma and Grandpa, and we all pile back in the

3

van, leaving our groceries behind. We drive the ten minutes home in silence, imagining what could cause Mom to be acting so weirdly. I glance at Gina and question with a look. She shrugs and raises her palms.

"Look at that, would you!" Mom barks, sounding pretty irritated. "Someone has parked right in the middle of our driveway! I'll have to park over here till I get them to move. Stay here in the warmth, everyone, and I'll come back and get us parked in the garage; no use all of us trudging through the snow and cold." She slams the door and heads across the road to our driveway.

Peering out my frosty side window in the late afternoon's descending darkness, I try to see who is blocking our way; it looks like maybe an RCMP cruiser to me. I feel a stab of sudden apprehension and listen to the dash clock ticking time off. Continuing to stare intently, I see three figures get out of that car and follow Mom inside.

"I think we should go in the house too, girls," my grandpa suggests calmly a few minutes later.

We all trudge mutely across the road, my runners crunching deep into the snow. *Mom's going to be mad at me for not wearing my Sorel boots*, I think blandly. We carefully climb our steep driveway.

Christmas lights twinkle from the rooftop, and our huge forest-cut Christmas tree fills the middle picture window. I chuckle, remembering our forest trek with Dad just three weeks ago to find that perfect specimen. It was so cold that Mom and my sisters retreated to the truck once we made our choice, but I stayed with Dad to the bitter end of shaking off the snow-laden branches and sawing the trunk. His moustache and eyebrows became frosted decorations on his cold-reddened face, and we laughed and pushed each other into the deep snow and continued to drag that chosen evergreen back to the truck.

As I take the last couple of steps up the driveway, I can see the fireplace is still burning—such a warm welcome. I hope Torr is OK, and I pray Dad comes home soon. I feel like something bad has happened and we need him with us.

4

Just as Grandpa reaches to open the front door, there's a wounded scream that seems to split me in half. Terrified, we enter and see Mom slipping down the wall, still in full-throated scream. I see Torr standing like a frozen statue by the kitchen table. Time stands still. I don't know what has happened and have no voice to ask.

Suddenly, just before totally collapsing, Mom jumps up and grabs the RCMP by his tie and repeats over and over, "Take me to him. Take me to him."

His intimidating size, his official uniform, and even his visible gun fail to deter her from her quest and strange command.

What is happening? Nothing is making sense, and my mind draws a blank.

The two persons with the RCMP are friends of ours and quietly assure Mom they will do as she asks, but their darting eyes tell me they're very hesitant and unsure about their promise.

I hear someone crying. I hear the log fire pop loudly. I hear my heartbeat thundering noisily in my ears. I feel Maggie brush by me and slip out the door, running away from this crazy scene. I wish I could run away.

To add to this sense of unreality, two more strange adults show up at our door and are welcomed in by the Mountie, who seems relieved to see them.

Maybe they are equipped to haul Mom away in a straitjacket to the looney bin. *Please Mom, be OK,* I plead silently. *We just need to call Dad and have him come straighten things out. He's always calm and strong. He'll look after us all.*

The two strangers herd us girls into the living room and near the fireplace while Mom appears to be leaving with our friends. Everything is happening too fast. The two strangers quietly and solemnly present each of us three girls with a teddy bear. I'm beginning to think the news is worse than can be imagined when one of the ladies very gently says, "I wish I didn't have to tell you this, but your dad is not coming home today. He was killed this afternoon

5

in an accident. Your grandma and grandpa and I are going to stay
with you till your mom gets back from the hospital."

My eyes open so wide I think they might fall out on the rug at
my feet. I just stare at the lady, who seems so small and weak with
red frizzy hair and sad brown eyes. Slowly but firmly, I give the teddy
bear back to her and head to my room, scooping up fluffy Borneo
on my way. I don't need a teddy bear. I need my dad!

Mom is finally back from the hospital—back from the morgue.
She's not screaming any more, at least. She is totally quiet and
just walking about like a wind-up toy. I want to ask her who will
drive me to Tosh's party, but our lives seem to be caught up in a
tornado.

I wish we were still a normal family. I want to turn back time to
before everything blew apart. Once things start flying around, there
is just no stopping the destruction, the vacuum, and eeriness. Eye of
the storm, I guess. Is there any solid ground? Can anything be saved?

I can't look at it.

I can't feel it.

I can't stop it.

Well, I am going to spend this tornado night at my friend's
house. I'm glad I have that to cling to—something normal.

I approach Mom gingerly. "Who can drive me to Tosh's place,
Mom? I think it's time I head over." Her blank stare chills me; it
seems she doesn't really see me.

I touch her arm gently and ask again.

She focuses on me and in a hoarse, scratchy voice, she tells me
that Tosh's mom has called and said I shouldn't come to the party.
It would upset everyone.

My one shred of hope is Ms Potter, my favourite teacher and
principal. She has somehow heard about this party and the ruckus
created by worried parents. So she is coming by our house shortly
to talk with Mom.

Our home seems to be filled with people, and as I glance around and see all the long faces, I catch snippets of hushed conversation.

"Such a terrible thing …"

"How old are the children …?"

"I heard about it while at the Safeway checkout line …"

"Can't get her to eat or drink anything …"

I feel like an outsider looking in. I decide to just retreat downstairs to the TV room and wait. How could anyone or anything come between me and my friends? This is silly. I try to think of some big, impressive words to describe our family right now, but my mind is failing me, so I choose to just wait and stare at the silent television.

I hear Mom coming down the stairs, and I hear the front door closing. Ms Potter is leaving, and I'm holding my breath, trying not to cry—not yet, at least. My mind is spinning, and I'm thinking of every argument I can use if needed. As I look at Mom and meet her eyes to gauge what's coming, I realize I don't recognize the person she is in this tornado. She looks old and pale, hunched inward, and she is wearing a baggy sweater that looks suspiciously like one of Dad's. Her eyes are puffy and red, and she's wearing Dad's favourite ball cap, pulled down low. I feel scared again.

Who is this battered-looking person in front of me? I wait, speechless, my arguments forgotten.

I'm holding my breath and waiting. Waiting for the *adult* verdict. Waiting for some strength and direction from Mom.

"You can go, honey." I see Mom's blank face and meet her dead eyes. She whispers hoarsely, "Ms Potter has spoken with all the parents and cleared it for you to still go. She will be back in half an hour and drive you over to Tosh's place." She turns and climbs slowly back up to the kitchen and the long faces there.

I feel I've been spared. *Thank you, Mom! Thank you, Ms Potter. Thank you, God! I can do this.*

Day 2, 29 December 1989

It's afternoon and I've just got home from Tosh's. I didn't want to come home, but Mom insisted I be here for the pastor's visit.

He is here now. We're scattered around the living room. Gina, still in her pyjamas, has snuggled Borneo in with her on the cushy chair near the fireplace. No one has lit it today. The drapes are still pulled. There are fresh flower arrangements on top of the piano, and three on the fireplace mantel. From my spot on the couch, wrapped in my only armour—Dad's warm favourite throw with cat silhouettes—I can see into the dining room, which is overflowing with more flowers. Through the dining room window, I can see snow gently falling.

It is so quiet.

Such silence!

I hope Pastor Harold has some answers for our many unanswerable questions. He's sitting in Dad's chair, wearing jeans and a sweater. His face is pale, and he's crossing and uncrossing his legs. I don't think he wants to be here either. We're ruining his Christmas too.

When he does speak, I don't hear him; I just see his lips moving.

I glance around the room at my family and wonder what they are thinking, hearing, feeling.

I don't think it's going well. Mom has that blank face I'm beginning to recognize. My sisters are very still, with eyes focused on the floor. I suspect, like me, they wish he hadn't come.

I know I believe in God. I believe in heaven. I just can't connect that with what is happening in our family right now.

Day 3, 30 December 1989

It's evening finally. Some of my cousins are here now, and we teens are going out for a few hours. That's great. We can block out the tornado for a while. We'll even include child sister Gina—so magnanimous of me.

Last night, all three of us girls slept together with Mom in the big brass bed. Even Borneo was there. *Did Mom even notice?* I wonder. She and Borneo have a love-hate relationship, and he has never been allowed in her bedroom before. Yet somehow he knew we needed him and just joined us uninvited!

Day 4, 31 December 1989—New Year's Eve Day

Sitting cross-legged on my unmade bed, flipping pages of a *Seventeen* magazine, unseeing, I think I hear the doorbell, and I vaguely discern voices drifting up from downstairs. Likely another floral arrangement. I don't want any in my room. I don't need any reminders. I glance out my window and see snow whirling in the wind. *Just like my churning guts*, I think miserably.

All I can really think about is Mom's insistence that all of us go to the viewing; she believes we need to see Dad one last time.

My mind pictures Josephine, our cat when we still lived in Macklin, flattened by a truck. We had a careful burial and remembering ceremony for her.

Dad ran into a train. *Will he be flattened like that?* I wonder. I just want him back! I don't want to see him any way but alive—fun and strong and being my ally. He understands me. He doesn't let me get away with things, but he is … my dad.

I'm refusing to go.

My hopeful read on the situation is that Mom won't insist. She doesn't have much of her usual zip.

Just as I relax, thinking the subject has been dropped, Mom knocks on my door.

"Can I come in?"

Before she can say anything more, I wrap my duvet tight around me and blurt out, "Mom, I don't want to go to a viewing. I can stay with Borneo or go to Tosh's place while you all go. I promise I will go to the funeral tomorrow." I threw in that promise in hopes it would give strength to my argument.

Mom's sitting beside me on the bed now. I hear her crying softly, and I see Borneo padding over to me from the hallway. I push him away fiercely. I want to push Mom away too.

"I know you don't want to go, hon. None of us do. It's something we have to do. It's something we *need* to do together." Refusing to look at her, I sit in silence. Finally, after what seems an age, I hear her say, "We leave in half an hour." And with a gentle shoulder squeeze, she leaves.

Perhaps I should have stuck to my guns and not gone to the viewing. In the end, I didn't even protest.

We arrive at the church, and someone ushers us to a small room, the "viewing room", and we enter reluctantly. Maybe I'm even the first one in. Maybe this is like *Alice in Wonderland* and I'm entering a total unknown. I certainly feel as if I've fallen through to nowhere or am suspended in space. But I can see clearly the huge, beautifully shining wood coffin. This is a sobering, hallowed space; it's just Mom, me and my sisters, and ... my dad.

Cautiously, noiselessly, we steal closer and closer, step by soundless step.

I feel as though I'm being sent to the principal's office. It's like the time our family spent a weekend in Edmonton to go to the Coliseum for an Oilers game and went shopping at West Edmonton Mall. I decided to try a stint of kleptomania, but Dad got suspicious about a certain purchase. I couldn't lie to Dad. He marched me right back to that store and security was called and punishment was discussed. Jail time? Death penalty? It was super scary, and worst of all, I had disappointed Dad. This viewing duty feels like worse punishment. *What am I being punished for this time?* I wonder.

I'm holding Mom's hand, and I'm closest to Dad's head, while Gina is clinging on the other side of Mom and Torr has gone to the other side of the coffin, right across from me. As we surround him, I pray silently that he feels and knows our love, wherever he is.

"Are his legs still on?" Gina blurts out. In this morbid silence of the viewing room, her question sounds like a shout to my sensitive ears. She's just turned eleven, but what a question. I don't hear Mom's answer.

"Can I touch him?" I try to ask, but I have no voice. It takes me three tries to get sound out.

"Yes," Mom boldly and simply replies.

I reach over and stroke the lapel of his tweed sports coat and then the silky feel of his dark burgundy tie, which looks so familiar against the bold check of his shirt, but I can't touch the pale, waxy-looking face or adjust his dark hair combed down over his forehead. I want to see his teasing, vivid blue eyes and wide smile.

"His hair looks funny, not like Dad's at all." I snarl critically.

I see his hands folded by his waist, revealing his wedding ring and his puzzle ring from their Thailand trip a couple of years back. His hands look tanned and strong with golden hairs—lifelike but without life.

"It really is Dad." I choke out the words in a strangled voice.

No one speaks after that.

I just hear our breathing marking the absence of his breath.

I find myself twisting the ring, which is still strange to my finger. It was Dad's wish to be the first man in our lives to give us a diamond on the Christmas we turned thirteen. I just got mine a week ago. Torr has had hers for two years already. Gina will get hers in two ... Yikes, she will never get hers now.

Dad is such a great gift giver, and we all love it. Mom says it takes all year to pay for it after Dad does his shopping. She always stresses about that, but I know she loves her bright yellow twelve-speed bicycle he gave her on their anniversary and the incredible ring she received from him on her last birthday. She had looked her entire life for a good birthstone ring, but aquamarine is often not very nice. This one is just exquisite. Yeah, Dad! You found it. What a romantic you are.

Who will give us Bernard Callebaut chocolate this Valentine's Day? Who will take us clothes shopping for our first-day-of-school outfits from now on? Who will watch the Oilers hockey games with us? Not Mom—that's for sure.

I wonder what Torr and Gina are thinking. What is Mom thinking?

I realize we are all crying.

We stay a long time. Where would energy or reason to leave come from? We do leave finally, empty-hearted. Empty. Empty.

When we get home from the viewing, I race upstairs to my room and slam the door with all my might. I know no one will be brave enough to disturb me—not even Borneo.

I collapse in the corner, hug my knees tightly, and try to collect my scattered life.

My thoughts travel back to our lively dinner discussion just a couple of weeks ago. Mom was working an evening shift, and I was on supper duty. I had forgotten to put the meatballs in the oven early enough, and they were rather rare. Dad covered for my error by declaring we'd eat them anyway. To ease the tension, I think, Torr mentioned that her social studies class had a discussion about the recent world news that the Berlin Wall had truly been abolished. We each had so many questions and suggestions and shared our sage wisdom, forgetting about the fear of death by salmonella from the undercooked meatballs!

"Why was it built in the first place?" started Gina. "How long is it, and how long did it take to build, and who built it?"

I knew Mom and Dad had been to Berlin and East Germany before we kids were born, and they spoke of the greyness and eeriness they felt during that visit.

Braving hearty bites of half-cooked meatballs, Dad managed to introduce a question into our raucous discussion. "What would life be like here in Fort Mack if a wall went through the city, separating two sections?" I remember seeing the hard hat ridge pressed into his dark hair at the end of the day and his bristly, ever-present moustache. The faint smell of crude oil from being on the active work sites clung to his greyish-green Nomex work clothes as the *gotcha* twinkle in his blue eyes gleamed at us.

I quickly answered, "Dad, it would be easy to accomplish here in Fort McMurray by just using the Athabasca and Clearwater Rivers as natural barriers; Thickwood and Timberlea would be on the north side, while Abasands, Grayling Terrace, downtown, Waterways, and us here in Beacon Hill would be on the south. We'd get the airport too."

Torr added, "It should be easy to create checkpoints like Checkpoint Charlie; just build an elaborate impassable gate manned with military guards at each end of the single bridge across the wide Athabasca. The bridge itself, plus the river, would serve as the equivalent of no man's land." I thought to myself that she looked pretty impressed with her own wisdom.

But Gina and I immediately saw an opportunity to get out of piano lessons, as our teacher was on the north and we lived on the south! Then Gina realized a possible problem.

"What if it was a Sunday, they enacted it all, and we were over in Thickwood at our cousin's place watching boring football?" she inserted, chin jutting and eyes ablaze. We all hated watching football.

Looking at Dad and raising my voice and eyebrows for emphasis, I added, "Like you *always* do, Dad, when Mom is working a Sunday shift at the hospital?"

"Guilty as charged", he conceded with a smile, a wink, and an elaborate wipe of his moustache with his napkin.

It was a sobering scenario though.

"Trapped over there, we wouldn't have access to grocery stores or the Peter Pond shopping mall. Highway 63, our only option for 'getting out of Dodge', so to speak, would be out of our reach, making travel and contact with extended family and friends impossible. Dad, you wouldn't be able to get to work, and … Mom would be able to get to our home, but we'd never be there!" I reasoned, tossing my napkin at him.

"Almost thirty years were imposed on the German folks," Torr added soberly.

"This extrapolation—I love that word: my word, not Tosh's, I add for proper credit—is rather terrifying."

"A split family!" we chorused.

"We'll always be family. No matter what happens," Dad said with firm conviction.

That's what we are now anyway—a split family. No Berlin Wall is needed. In a split second, the tornado has accomplished the same horror.

Tomorrow will be the funeral. I've never been to a funeral.

Mom has arranged for each of us to have someone in the family sit with us and look out for us. I guess she is not able; she's too broken, I think.

I get Auntie Beth, Gina gets Cousin Natalia, and Torr gets Aunt Rhoda.

Day Five, 1 January—New Year's Day

The service is sorta nice. The hundreds of people present and their singing are buoying me up. It feels as if it is prolonging something. I don't want it to ever end. I would just be caught up in the roar of the tornado again, dropped back into chaos and confusion. In my mind, I hear again Mom's unending wounded scream and see her sliding down the wall before attacking the RCMP with her demands. I want to scream too. I have demands too. Maybe that would let out some of my confusion.

I don't hear the speakers; I just watch their mouths moving and try to settle the racing thoughts and images travelling around inside my head. I hear over and over again the red-haired lady saying, "Your dad won't be coming home tonight."

The trouble with this tornado is that there is no root cellar or bomb shelter to flee to for protection. I remember that when we still lived in Macklin, a tornado went through Dad's work site and a plank was driven right through a trucker's windshield without even shattering the glass, just moments after the driver had sought refuge in the office. The plank would have impaled him if he had still been in the truck. I looked up the meaning of "impaled" when I overheard that story—pretty gory stuff. Well, this unseen tornado is pretty gory too, and I feel impaled.

I try to avoid looking at the coffin. It's closed up now, and silently I ask, "Dad, are you really in there? I want you to know Mom chose a grand and shiny wooden casket for you, and you looked really handsome, except for the way they combed your hair. I'm sorry I wasn't brave enough to touch your hair and try to fix it properly. I'm wearing the outfit we bought together for my first day of school this year. Remember? It's a deep-wine-coloured, calf length bibbed skirt, with really wide shoulder straps, and a long-sleeved shirt with fine grey stripes that goes with it. I wear it a lot, but especially today to honour you. I don't know what else to do, Dad. Please don't be gone for good."

When we get home from the funeral, I help Grandma and Grandpa carry in the varied floral arrangements, and then I escape, unnoticed, to my room.

I feel like a wet dishrag, and I'm cold and shivering all over. If life were still normal, Grandpa would probably be saying to me, "You look like you've been dragged through a knothole backwards!"

I change into my soft mock turtleneck, one of Dad's gifts just a week ago, and pyjama bottoms, and I crawl under my warm down duvet.

Eventually I quit shaking and just lie listening to the soft hum of a houseful of people and let my mind wander.

I liked the ride in the limousine. I smile as I think how funny it is that it came late to pick us up. We didn't want to go anyway, and the funeral surely wouldn't start without us, so there wasn't any fuss about waiting on it. I liked all the family meeting us at the church, and I liked being ushered in special-like to our reserved place at the front of the church.

Again I think of the wonderful peace I felt from the hundreds of voices singing during the service, but I felt robbed, missing Dad's strong lead voice.

I almost got the giggles remembering Dad's god-awful, earth-shattering sneezes that often interrupted church services. How mortifying for us girls. I'd give anything to hear one of those now.

It was weird seeing so many strangers. These strangers knew Dad. His life was way bigger than just him and me, and that feels strange somehow.

I liked the luncheon time after the funeral; everyone seemed less morbid and was just having a good time. I could block out what had really happened.

I didn't like strangers hugging me or the things they said.

"I know what it's like, honey," said one hefty stranger who smelled of cigarette smoke and had a pudgy double chin. I wanted to scream back, "So you know how I feel. Your dad died suddenly from a train accident when you were a thirteen-year-old girl and never got to say goodbye!"

"You'll be OK," comforted a stylish young woman with layers of make-up, stilettos, and a business suit.

"You know I'll be OK because …?" I wanted her to continue with her reasoning.

"At least you still have your mom," stated a lady I recognized from church, as if that had anything to do with anything.

I wanted to grill her. "Yeah, at least my mom is still here. How long will that last? And she's rather vacant these days. Does that still count?"

Most of all, I didn't like the feeling of finality when our friends carried him out of the church, right past me.

I couldn't stop it.

I couldn't believe it.

I couldn't change it.

It was good I had Auntie Beth to walk me out following that procession of finality. My legs were jelly, my chest was tight, and I felt faint.

Dad, please don't go; don't leave me. I'll be a perfect daughter. I won't throw soup cans at Gina or ever use bad language. I won't leave my room a mess or be late for curfew. I won't hand assignments in late or harass the teachers. I won't forget to cook the meatballs the right length of time. I won't ... I can't think of any more sins right now.

Day 6, 2 January 1990

Today is burial day. It is terribly wintry. We travel many hours from Fort McMurray in a howling blizzard to bury Dad in his home-grown territory. Fate of all fates, we get trapped at the railway tracks in Vermilion, just north of the cemetery. It is an unending train that mocks us mercilessly, jockeying back and forth, grumbling and banging left and then right as if undecided which way to go. We all sit in our own silence, transfixed, each with his or her own thoughts. I worry Mom might come unglued and start howling again and collapse like the afternoon they told her about the accident, the train, Dad ...

That was an afternoon forever etched on my mind's video. I now know that as I was racing to catch the phone that day and Mom was ironing Dad's jeans in the hallway and cautioning me to be careful, he was at that very moment colliding with the train.

Now here we all are, suspended in time and silence, just us in a horror film—us and the mocking train. It seems like hours but is likely only twenty minutes.

I'm impressed with my family and friends. They have waited and waited, not knowing how late we would be getting here. We have forged through the poor road conditions and endured the eight-hour drive. It's one hundred degrees below zero, the snow is deep, and the unrelenting wind bites us with a vengeance, but here they are beside us at the graveyard. We are numb from the tornado, so it's easy for us, but they are still nice, normal families that still feel and think. How can they manage? I hang back from the group and stand under an evergreen tree, but someone has an arm around my shoulders, trying to protect me from that wind. *Thanks.* I wish that arm could protect me from the tornado too. I watch the quiet procession as six of our trusted family carry Dad in the big wooden box. It is a long walk from the cars to the gravesite in deep, beautiful snow. I can see Mom now, beside the coffin, standing alone, her head bowed and almost totally hidden in her long, hooded fur. Torr is a splash of blue colour among blacks and greys in her long winter coat and supported by our friend Barb from Calgary. I don't see Gina at the moment. I hope someone is protecting her.

A pastor I don't know says a few words and a prayer and invites everyone to the Wainwright church for a luncheon.

There is no singing; it is too cold.

I see Mom pluck the wide blue ribbon from the new multitude of flowers covering the coffin. Folks are choosing single flowers as mementos, I guess. I don't want one.

I want Dad. Is he really in that beautiful wooden box to be lowered into the silent, cold earth once we leave?

The days keep coming. Casseroles keep coming. Family and friends take turns staying with us. We are back in school. Kids ask horrible questions.

"Did his head come off in the accident?" I don't remember my answer.

"Are you moving away?"

"Did you see the cool picture in the paper of the accident?"

After a couple of days, everything was back to normal and there were no more questions. That feels worse than the horrid questions because I'm not back to normal. At thirteen, I know how important being normal is.

I am the drama queen in our home and love being in the city drama group. But now I want to quit. I'm being pressured to complete the show by the director, of course, and Tosh. She wants me to stay in it because she is "Daddy Roebuck's secretary" in the play and we've had so much fun till now.

Even Mom expects me to do it. I stand my full height, knowing I'm already a couple of inches taller than her, throw my shoulders back, lift my chin for even more height, and tell her, "If Dad can't be here to watch, I don't want to do it any more."

My effort didn't even make a dent in her reasoning. It's easiest to not fight everyone and just do it. I know that after it's done in March, *I will not do drama again*!

Mom doesn't work on her beautiful cross-stitch project, and I never hear her singing any more. She doesn't go to the pool any more, and she quit the volleyball league. Now she just bundles up and walks the Beacon Hill perimeter over and over.

Answering the phone, I take a call from a lady.

"Mom, it's Jennifer with your volleyball team!" I call out.

"I can't come to the phone right now; just tell her I'll call back."

When I hang up, I find Mom cleaning the upstairs bathroom in preparation for Grandma and Grandpa coming back tomorrow, and I tell her of an earlier call.

"Mom, Shelly called from the hospital while you were out

walking and wants you to call her back too—about scheduling shifts, I think."

"Oh brother," Mom says with a heavy sigh, and she begins rubbing the mirror harshly. "I wish they'd quit calling," she says, and she tosses the cleaning cloth on the floor. "Both of them. I just can't go back to work, and I have no interest in volleyball either."

"Maybe you'd have fun at volleyball with your team and work might … might be interesting," I stutter, trying out the role of mothering my mother.

"Thanks, hon," she says, and she finally looks at me directly. "But I never sleep, and my mind is all over the place or in neutral. I wouldn't be a safe nurse working in the ER or ICU right now. I wish they understood that." She wilts into a heap, sitting on the tub. Then, in a soft voice, she asks with her head still down, resting on her hands, "Please go and transfer the clothes to the dryer for me, will you?"

"Sure, Mom," I say, and I escape, not wanting to hear any more about her tornado life. I wish I could turn back time. I don't know how to live in this.

It's looking like none of us do.

None of us are skating any more. Torr quit a year ago for health reasons anyway, and Gina and I have just faded out since the tornado. We don't seem to be going for our piano lessons yet either. That I don't mind!

Torr, who has quit everything, is the family beauty queen. Her massive head of hair in shades of light fall halfway down her back, and her big blue eyes and flawless skin are hard to compete with— quite a contrast to my dark curls and dark eyes

Torr never seems to get in trouble.

She could rile Dad, though, with arguments about women's lib. I think he just liked to egg her on. Unlike Torr, I'm usually in some kind of trouble. Maybe that's why I was Dad's favourite.

I admire Torr, though. She's fun and brave. It's a year and a half since she got sick—some kidney thing called IGA nephropathy.

That's a great word for my linguistic fetish. Torr has given up her skating and her dream of ice dancing at the Olympics. She misses half of her school days. (I wouldn't mind that!) She's had to make big decisions about whether to take medication with ugly side effects, and she had a painful kidney biopsy.

She's beautiful, brave, and buoyant, but now she never goes out with her friends.

As I take the stairs two at a time down to the laundry room, by the kitchen to do as Mom asked, I see Torr sitting at the dining room table, writing away.

"Hey, whatcha doin' sis? Homework?"

"Nope, trying to write a few thank-you cards. So many people have been so helpful and generous these last few weeks. And, truly, I can't seem to stay focused on any school stuff anyway," she laments, the final words fading away quietly.

"Well, you sound like Mom, Torr. Hey, do you think she will go back to work soon?" I ask brightly, changing the subject. I need to feel my big sis is coping just fine.

"I think she's just trying to look after us and avoid everything and everyone else," Torr states.

"Maybe," I reply thoughtfully. "I'd better get the wash transferred. Maybe I will make some half-cooked meatballs for supper and help Mom out. I sure miss the meals the church ladies were bringing every day for a while." I head determinedly to the laundry room, wondering where our little sister is. Maybe she'll help me concoct some supper.

Our little sister, Gina, is a fashion queen in my mind—the ever-reliable fashion judge. Now, Miss Fashion doesn't voice any opinions. Even her best bosom-buddy, Maggie, gets ignored most of the time. Those two have been inseparable all the time we've been here in Fort Mack.

Gina is also manager of everything. She's always right and never gives up. She's a negotiator guru, and Mom says she'd make an excellent lawyer. She and Mom seem to enjoy the duelling, but I think Gina usually wins. Lucky brat! I don't even engage in the duels. I'd never win. I never even win a coin toss.

I haven't won this duel about quitting drama either.

"So why can't I quit my drama group?" I reason with Mom. "Everyone else has quit everything. It's not fair."

"Life is not always about fair," Mom replies, as always.

Well, that's for sure for me anyway. I'll just sit in the garden and eat worms. Or maybe I'll call Tosh and go for a sleepover at her house. Again I think, *What would my life be without friends?*

March 1990

It's finally March, and tonight is my final performance as Miss Hannigan. The rehearsals have been fun, and for last night's performance, Mom, my sisters, and Grandma and Grandpa came.

"You were great, N. C.," Torr had said after curtain call as she grabbed me, hugged me, and gave me a huge bouquet of brilliant flowers, from all the family. I'm proud of you, Miss *Hannigan!* Could I have your autograph on my programme? And a picture beside you?" She pulled me to her side once again as she handed the camera to her friend. I smelled the fragrance of her shampooed long hair swinging by me as we got ourselves positioned. Her closeness and her words of praise buoyed me up.

Lots of folks clamoured around similarly, and I felt special— famous, even. Mom was nowhere in sight, and I asked Torr where she was.

"You know she avoids people now. She left as the curtain fell. She said she'd wait in the car for us."

I was disappointed but not surprised. She still keeps the drapes closed most days and goes out only when she has to, except for her many walks around the Beacon Hill perimeter—and that still scares me; will she always make it back?

"Torr, a few times, during the performance, I caught a glimpse of a tall, dark-haired man in a sports coat and immediately thought it was Dad," I say in a whisper.

"Oh, N. C., those glimpses happen to me too. Are you OK?"

"Expecting to hear his congratulations and get his bear hug leaves me feeling so empty without it," I admit while I accept her comforting hug.

Tonight I have no family in the audience.

However, as my first scene begins, I hear an ungodly sneeze in the huge darkened theatre, and I'm sure Dad is out there. I hear his clapping, louder than others', and at final curtain call there is a loud fingers-in-mouth whistle. Dad taught me how to do that whistle. Mom can't do it. Torr and Gina can't do it. Only Dad and I can do it.

The curtain falls one last time, and I fold up in a heap, still hearing that whistle in my head, and let the tears fall unchecked.

It's still March.

Mom turns forty. My cousin Natalia and her family live here, and she's Mom's best friend. Though she is quite a bit younger than Mom, it doesn't seem to affect their closeness. They even have a small home business together—Wishful Thinking. But that has ended too since the tornado.

"Mom, are you actually going out tonight, you and Natalia?

"Indeed I am. Aren't you proud of me? Not sure which restaurant, but I will call you when I get there. Victoria will be home with you, and Gina is overnight at Maggie's. I won't be gone long; I promise."

"Mom, we'll be fine. Please be careful," I say as my mind automatically switches to worry mode. "Do you have your wallet?" I prattle on as I glance around the room, looking for her purse.

She snatches up her bag, slings it over a shoulder, gives me a smirk, and admits, "Noelle-Cheri, I know I have been forgetful and

I haven't been very social, and I admit I would rather not go tonight either, but I think it means a lot to Natalia. I get that it's my birthday, but that just means I'm getting older … without your dad."

"Like me doing *Annie*," I say, seeing the parallel. "An important event but without him."

Mom nods and turns to watch out the living room window for her expected ride. I'm not sure she sees the parallel, and I sigh.

"You look pretty, Mom," I add as she heads out the front door.

"Thanks, sweetheart. Goodbye."

We're careful to say "goodbye" and not "see you". "See you" is not guaranteed, and not getting to say goodbye is appalling. I know.

It's still March.

Mom loved her gentle surprise party. She came home and told us all about it.

It seemed a good time to prod Mom about our hopeful trip to California. We know we have been invited to join our aunt and uncle on their way back from some Mission trip. Torr, Gina, and I see it as an easy decision. Mom, however, is stuck in the mud—or should I say stuck in the snow.

"Are we really going to join Aunt Rhoda and Uncle Edward in California during Easter break?" I ask nonchalantly. I'm not sure how to spell "nonchalantly", but I love the word.

"Noelle-Cheri, do we have to talk about that now? I'm tired. Exhausted actually."

"But it's just a couple of weeks away," I persist, while giving my sisters a meaningful stare to get them on board with this pressure.

"Mom, didn't you say there are lots of air miles we can use from all Dad's business travel?" Gina asks, wading in.

"And Gina has never been to Knotts Berry Farm," adds Torr rather weakly.

That wasn't much of a power-punch argument, I think in disgust, slanting a look at her.

Mom's shoulders sag, and she lets out a long sigh, turns quietly away from us, and begins putting on her winter armour. She's obviously retreating to the trails, and we let her go out into the cold, dark night, hidden in her long, hooded fur coat, a scarf covering her face like a burka, puffy leather mitts, and her bulky Sorel boots. She is just a dark, shadowy figure that will soon be covered in frost but will, we hope, return to us.

We stand in silence a few moments.

"Sorry, N. C.; I couldn't think of anything persuasive," laments Torr.

"Do you think Mom will still agree to go yet?" Gina asks

"Who knows," I respond in defeat. Then, raising my voice and looking towards the front door as if yelling back at Mom, I shout, "I hope you know you can't hide on the snowy trails forever!"

Just two days later, to my happy surprise, Mom tells us she used Dad's air miles to get flights for us all from Fort Mack to Edmonton, then first class to Vancouver, and finally on down to Los Angeles to meet up with Auntie and Uncle for a week at Disney. How exciting—a break from the endless Fort Mack winter! Not too shabby for a bunch of orphans.

That's what the kids at school call us now, and I again remembered James, from my class, just yesterday, call, "Hey, N. C., our little orphan, can you help me with my book report?"

"Well, *Jughead James,* no, I can't," I sassed right back at him, and we laughed.

"Mom, are we really orphans now?" I later ask hesitantly, fearing the answer.

"That's a hard question, hon. I think it usually refers to both parents dying. Regardless, Noelle-Cheri, we'll always be a family, no matter what." She states this firmly, turning to look at me directly.

Crazy. Those are the exact words Dad said a week before his accident, when we imagined the Berlin Wall happening in Fort Mack!

"Dad, it doesn't feel like family any more without you." I try to hear his voice in my head, repeating his assurance. My throat and chest feel tight, and I squeeze back tears.

I don't feel like we're still a family, I admit to myself. *I need Dad to complete my understanding of family.*

Before school on Monday, I can't find Mom anywhere.

"Gina, do you know where Mom is?" I call out as she passes my bedroom door.

She hesitates and then enters my domain, plunks down crossed-legged on the rug, and offers, "I think she's out on the trails again. What do you need?" She looks up at me with a question in her eyes, resting her head on her hands.

I hear Torr bounding up the stairs, and she joins in our conversation. "Am I missing something?" she enquires from the doorway, looking at us hard.

"I just had a question for Mom and wondered where she was, but Gina says she headed out walking the perimeter trails again."

"No surprise there," Torr adds, sounding ticked, and she comes over and sits on the edge of my bed, still in her robe, her hair looking wild.

"What's with all the trail walking, do you think, guys?" I ask.

"Well, she and Dad used to do that a lot after we were gone to bed. Remember?" Gina says. "Mom told me she feels close to God when she walks the trails." As she is speaking, she welcomes intruder Borneo to her lap. I guess he doesn't want to miss out on our family discussion either.

"I worry she wants to walk into the trees and never return," I risk sharing

"Perhaps her experience of the owl, comforting her that first frigid night on the trail, entices her back to the woods again and again," Torr utters. "She told me that single owl visit calmed and comforted her briefly, and that it felt like Dad, by some miracle, was saying a goodbye and an I love you. Maybe it's a good thing she does these walks."

I tune out and chew on that explanation a while as Torr and Gina continue without me.

"Maybe you're right, Torr," I allow, and I reach for that hope. "But I often think about what would happen to us if Mom was gone too."

"I worry about that as well", confesses Gina.

"Let's just pray that doesn't happen," Torr says with a sigh.

I don't feel reassured.

It's still March.

Some people think of March as the herald of spring. I don't see any signs. The snow is so high it just falls back down when you try to throw it off the driveway. One fellow from the church youth group has faithfully kept it shovelled for us since the tornado. This constant snow reminds me of the fun I had with Dad just a few months ago while getting our Christmas tree. Again I see his moustache and eyebrows, a frozen monument to the escapade.

And then there are those other evergreen boughs—the ones on Dad's casket. The florists in Fort Mack were so short of supplies because of Christmas demands and so many arrangement requests that they didn't have much for us to choose from. Mom thought natural evergreen boughs would be the best solution, and I think Fritz and Uncle Tony secured the appropriate and cherished branches directly from the forest. We had big, wide ribbons with our names on them entwined through the branches. It was so beautiful. It was so fragrant. It was the sight and smell of living things.

June 1990

My life is about to change again, and I can't find a way to stop it.

School will be out in a couple of weeks, our trip to Disney a small and distant haze.

Mom is talking about moving us away from Fort Mack.

"Mom, I think we should definitely stay right here in Fort Mack," I say with conviction, stamping a heavy foot right in the middle of the kitchen.

"It's not a place for our kind of family, and there is no reason to stay," she counters bluntly.

Our kind of family—how freaky. What kind of family is that? I wonder. *Not the nice or normal kind, but the moving kind, I guess. The "orphan" kind! The not-with-a-big-company kind? The unemployed kind?*

Of course, no one asks me. I'm the only one who wants to stay.

And what about that "no reason to stay" comment?

"Tosh is here. Jenna is here. Megan, Celeste, and Erin are here— just to name a few reasons. Who will I hang with after we move? That's five good reasons right there!" I say furiously and stomp off to my room!

Why should I start all over? It's senseless and moronic.

"Torr," I say, grabbing her arm as we meet on the stairs, "how can Mom make such a silly decision?"

"What silly decision, sis?" she asks, halting on the stairs.

"You know, moving away from here!" I snarl impatiently and in disgust, flinging my arm around to gesture to our home.

"N. C., what if it is a good decision?" she challenges quietly.

"How can that be? This is our home. This is where our friends are. This is where we still have a feeling of Dad." Surprised at my own vulnerable words, I turn and rush to my room. Then I turn back and sling, "Maybe everyone is just running away!"

How can Torr and Gina be glad about this? Even Borneo seems ready to go. For a feline, he's as smart as they come, but I bet Gina's been brainwashing him. Wait till he realizes it means an eight-hour drive in the motor home, probably in his cage up on the front bunk. I should remind him how well he tolerates the short trip to the vet every few months for his shots and things. *Psycho Borneo, think about that. If you will place your vote with mine, then I just need to swing one more to win.* Of course, that assumes a democracy, and it seems democracy comes and goes with convenience.

Cousin Natalia and Fritz and their girls, Allie and Trish, are here. What will Mom do without them? All our church friends are here. We'll miss their help and friendship. Why move someplace else? Our picnic spots are here, along with Gregoire Lake camping. I recall the sound of Dad's truck in the driveway and his teasing voice calling up the stairway, "I'm home. Who's got supper ready?"

And what happens next fall—a new school? What will that be like? Not to my liking, I know. What will keep Dad in our today with everything new and changing? *Where are you, Dad? Sometimes I dream that you're just away on business like we're used to and you'll just call from the airport and we'll all go pick you up like we always did. We'll be mad at you for being away so long, but we'll be so glad that you're back; we'll forgive you.*

What do you think about that? Please come back.

Only silence answers me.

The farewell parties are thankfully all over. The sleepovers, unfortunately, are also all over—done. The cute gifts and cards have been received and tucked away.

I'm making a lacklustre (a great word to share with Tosh) attempt to finish packing up my room. I don't want to pack. I don't want to leave. I want to stay here. *Dad, this is our home with you,* I say in my mind. *This is your looney piggy bank that I often stole from. It goes with me for sure.*

"I can see you sitting in your home office, behind that monstrous desk, right across from my room, with your *Mulroney* reading glasses on that we liked to tease you about." I collapse on my bed and let the tears spill over unrestrained; I just can't always keep them away.

And through the blur of my tears, I see that teeny golden golf bag, complete with five teeny-weeny removable golf clubs I gave you on your birthday last summer. Now they're mine—not much to have of you. I wish, I wish … I wish I could turn back time and see your constant pride in me and hug you once more at least.

Thursday has arrived. The moving truck is full, and our Olds 98 is attached.

Here we stand in our driveway, in the shade of our tall house. I look up at Dad's home office window and imagine I see a shadowy figure. My breath catches, and I give a start as my young cousin throws her little arms around my legs. Natalia, Fritz, and their kids are here for final goodbyes. Maggie is here too for a last goodbye to Gina and all of us. She's been like another member of our family for three years and was a witness to the horrible day of the tornado. She's so cute, tiny like a doll, and very quiet today. Gina has loyal friends.

Tosh couldn't be here today, and I'm glad. I don't think I could leave if she were here to hold me back.

As the four of us cling to all their love and reality, we just can't break away and get in that motor home. I knew we shouldn't do this. I think we should just cancel the moving truck quickly, before they get out of town. *We can't really be doing this. Please, God. Help.*

"Dad, where are you? I don't want to leave you."

Here, I still imagine, every day, that I hear your truck in the driveway when getting home after work. I can imagine you calling to us as you come in the front door. I feel a bubbly laugh down deep as I remember you teasing Natalia's little girl, Trish, saying, "Hey, little Gunk," while tossing her high in the air and making her giggle and squeal every time. I bet that's how you treated me when I was little.

I hear Dad's clear assurance: "We will always be a family, N. C."

Somehow we load into that motor home, all wailing unrestrainedly.

Only Borneo is silent, partly because we sedated him and partly because he's used to our grief and is a good counsellor. As the miles go by, we're still crying. We don't often cry together any more, but this has put us all over the brink at the same time, so we share our loss through mutual tears. We are leaving our life behind. Are we leaving Dad behind?

The trip drags on endlessly. I've heard a quote in the past, from the Bible somehow, that "with God, a day is as a thousand years." Well, I can identify with that. It's been at least a thousand years since Dad left. I can't say "since he died". I don't ever want to say that. We all live in this purgatory bubble, staggering along with no real plan.

But hey, I will try to envision our new home. Mom says it's a bungalow, not a two-storey like we're used to. The garage is not attached like we're used to. It's an older house than we're used to, but it has been newly renovated, so we don't have to do anything to it. There is no air-con, but Mom thinks the huge trees in front will shade the whole house from the summer heat, and there is an apple tree in the back. Mom evaluates real estate by how many trees come with the house! There is room for our motorhome and our trampoline near the garage, which is on a lower level than the house. I can't really picture it yet—maybe because I don't want to. I want to keep things the way they used to be.

Fall 1990

Summer is over. Our new place is definitely nestled in among gigantic black poplars in the front and crab apple trees in the back like Mom said; this gives it a protected feel. Though it is smaller than the one we had in Fort Mack, Mom says it is paid for with money from Dad's life insurance, and the government give a monthly stipend till we girls each turn twenty-one, if still in university. That sounds like forever away.

I have my own room—essential. It's definitely much smaller

than my room in Fort Mack—yuck. It has new plush carpet, though, in an ocean-green colour, and my gauzy white curtains from Fort Mack came with me, as well as my pastel plaid duvet cover. The oval mirror on my small antique dresser reflects Dad's looney piggy bank and miniature golf set wherever I am in the room; it almost feels like home.

I share a bathroom with Gina, as her bedroom is right next to mine and not much bigger, but it is big enough for her double bed. Torr has a big room in the basement and her own bathroom, lucky duck.

Mom's room is right across the hall from me, and she has French doors to the huge deck, which houses a hot tub. That's the big project she initiated as soon as we unpacked. I think Mom has been more energetic and less morbid since we moved. Maybe distance has hidden some of our pain. Maybe a new start is good for us all.

My weeks at summer camp, have been fun, and no one hassled me about being an orphan. Dad's voice and stories are always with me, though, and I miss him. His childhood story of riding with his grandpa, who spit tobacco all over his window and said, "Gosh darn, Quinnie, I thought that window was down!" always cracks me up as I visualize Dad mimicking his grandfather chewing and spitting sideways.

"Girls!" I hear Mom calling from the kitchen.

"Coming!" I call back as my feet hit the carpet. Everywhere in this house is sea green and dusty rose, but the kitchen has a sunshine ceiling, light wood cabinets, and a big window to look out on the deck and treed yard. Mom is making supper, and it smells wonderful.

"I have news for you guys," she begins. I feel uneasy awaiting the announcement, but nothing could have prepared me for this news.

It seems our family is about to change some more.

Over the summer, while home briefly many times, I met family friends that dropped in to cheer Mom up. Now it seems one is going to marry her! Is this a good thing? Mom thinks so.

We went to his wife's funeral some months ago; it was after our trip to California, I think. I sort of remember seeing them occasionally over the years. She was such a nice lady, and we had fun when we visited them on their dairy farm. We rode ponies and watched the boys try to ride calves. They don't have a dairy farm any more, just a beef cattle farm. I haven't seen them much over the last few years while isolated in Fort Mack, but I knew they were the people to look after us if Mom and Dad died. They are obviously people Mom and Dad trust and admire.

Well, Dad is dead! There, I said it. I don't believe it, though.

It could happen to Mom too, so it seems fitting to connect with this family, but are we really going to become a blended family? My thoughts are tumbling around every which way, and it seems hard to breathe normally.

I'm trying to recall seeing him over the summer and my impressions. He was tall, I remember—even taller than Dad—with dark, curly hair and big-framed glasses, and I liked his strong greeting hug. We get so many hugs these days since the tornado, and I like that.

Mom looks happy, chatting so upbeat. I'll have two brothers, I realize. And ... I'll have a new dad. No, not a new dad—never a new dad!

"He's always wanted a daughter," I hear Mom say, continuing her spiel, trying to sell this news.

"Well, what does that have to do with anything?" I ask as this catches my attention. "He'd be getting three of us!" I add in my snarling, disapproving voice.

"Will we move to their farm?" Gina asks, sounding unconvinced.

"Girls, I know this must seem strange, and I know there are lots of questions. I don't have many answers yet. Just trust me for now"

"But what about Dad?" I hurl at her mercilessly with flashing eyes and my chin raised, ready for a fight.

Silence stretches long as I continue to glare.

Then, quietly, with a sheen of tears in her eyes, Mom takes hold of my hand and places it over my heart and then hers. "Your dad is always and forever in here, but he is gone. We have to live without him. None of us like it. I can't fix it. No one can, Noelle Cheri."

"Well, this is crazy!" I state, snatching my hand back. "Why didn't you die instead of Dad?!" I hurl at her.

I gulp, and I hear my sisters gasp at my cruelty as I storm off to my room in a fury, not caring who gets hurt and forgetting about the supper that was smelling so great just minutes ago.

Later that night, I learn from Torr that *he's* going to be in town for the coming weekend. *Maybe I can be away somewhere*, I think hopefully.

I've had a few days to digest the news, and pulling from my brief days on stage, I decide to play the gracious role of a dutiful daughter, sweet and charming.

I hear a car in the front driveway. My heart speeds up, and I take a big gulp of air.

Listening to Mom's and Torr's voices of greeting, I hear his deep voice but can't make out words from my room.

Gina barges in and suggests we make an entrance together.

"Good idea, Gina," I say with relief in my voice.

Feeling saucy in my blue jean cut-offs and my red *Annie* production T-shirt, with my long, wavy hair up in a scrunchie, I follow Gina, and we make our grand entrance.

His being two steps down from me, still standing in the entrance, places him almost at eye level with me, so I offer a confident hello. His brief "Hello, Noelle" makes me suspect he is as uncomfortable meeting us as we are meeting him again, under these new circumstances.

"Well, we'd better get going," he says. "Paul and Cynthia are meeting us at the Black Knight restaurant." He adds firmly, with the briefest of glances over us girls, "They're just expecting the two of us."

Mom's smile disappears, and she looks to be about to counter that statement, but she then turns to us and says, "Girls, I'll just be a couple of hours and—"

"That's no problem," I interrupt, glad to have this meeting over with. "I was just about to take a book and jump in the hot tub anyway. See you later!"

As the car backs out of the driveway, we stand huddled together and I high-five my sisters, feeling relieved.

"Well, that went well, I'd say. Short and sweet."

"Feels really strange," Gina adds. "How come we weren't invited along? I bet the boys are more fun."

"They're pretty old now," Torr guesses with a thinking frown. "Through school at least. They won't likely be interested in adding little sisters to their home."

"Why is Mom getting married anyway?" Gina asks simply, looking first at Torr and then me. Getting no immediate answer, she shrugs and starts to walk away.

"She must believe this will be good for us all," Torr suggests. Maybe it's her attempt to go on with life. I don't know. Maybe it's like when she finally made herself open our drapes and let the world exist again for us. Maybe it's just plain trying to run away from everything?"

I don't want to talk about it or think about it all any more, so I turn, grab my book, and get my suit on for the hot tub, just as I had said.

A week has gone by, and I'm a bit excited to be heading to the farm. What a long drive. Seems to be more than three hours to me. There's no farmhouse apparently, so they actually live in town. Sounds sensible to me. Best of both worlds.

"We're here," says Mom as we pull into a long driveway. The house is weathered looking and big with lots of windows, but all the drapes are closed to the world. It reminds me of Mom shutting the world out after our tornado in a similar way.

We all hesitate while getting out of the vehicle, as if scared of something. I'm scared the boys will be as unfriendly as the dad. I'm scared my life is changing too fast. I'm scared I will lose Dad's voice in my head.

On the second ring of the doorbell, we are invited in. It is very dark and cluttered, and I see the boys are dressed for farming, ready to go. We have farm clothes with us too, including gum boots, so we change quickly.

"Torr and N. C., come ride with us," one of the boys invites, and we pile into their red sports car. I don't even see Mr Kreiger. Things are looking up. This is really fun. Tunes are blaring, and they laugh and joke with us. This must be what having brothers is all about. I forget about Gina, relegated to riding with Mom and Mr Kreiger in the farm truck.

The day went by in a blur of new experiences: watching a new calf get its wobbly feet stabilized under it, climbing all over the huge stacks of straw bales, and riding on the tractor with the boys. I did have a bit of a scare and received a frown from Mr Kreiger when an animal got past me while we were herding a bunch into a different field. My waving arms and shouting didn't work, and in my excitement, I stepped in you-know-what. Gross! My new gum boots were all yucky. Everyone was laughing but me.

On the long ride home to Red Deer, late into the night, we all talk about the day and the future, hoping to keep Mom awake.

"I hope we move up there," Gina says. "I like the farm."

"Me too," I add. "Riding in that forklift basket was crazy, and the boys were a lot of fun to be around. Cleaning my boots was not a lot of fun."

"I knew I could smell something," Mom teases me.

"Ha ha," I respond, rolling my eyes.

"The little calves were hilarious," Torr says with laughter in her voice. "Jumping around on stiffened legs like wind-up toys. And their curly hides so fuzzy and cute. That newborn was the highlight though!"

None of us voice how we feel about Mr Kreiger.

Tomorrow we are going dress shopping. That might be fun. I'm always up for new clothes. I love this bigger city and the fun shops.

Leaving the dress shop, I'm grateful to be back in my jeans and sunny yellow T-shirt. I pull my ball cap down over my eyes a tad to hide my disappointment. Mom chose purple dresses for us. It is a royal colour, I'll give you that, but all three of us girls in so much purple just does not do it for me!

Now back in my room, I use the sliding mirror doors on my wardrobe to help me adjust to wearing the dress. My sisters waltz in, and we sashay around, mimicking a catwalk event till we collapse on my narrow bed in a jumble of purple lace and convulsive hysterics.

Staring up at my teardrop chandelier sparkling in the sun's rays flooding my room, I press my hands on my stomach to ease the pain from laughing so hard and look sideways to see my sisters in similar straits.

I manage to say, "If laughter and tears are God's healing gifts, like Mom always says, then we should be in good health today!"

Torr voices her thoughts. "It's Mom's wedding, and I think it's cool we get to be her bridesmaids."

"Yeah, and it gives a diversion to the loneliness of this new place and the big junior high school I'm trying to navigate," I note as laughter gives way to seriousness and my mind wanders. No one here knows our family. No one here knew my dad and how fun he was helping out at Friday family gym nights at our school back in Fort Mack. My heart hurts.

I hear Gina voice her opinion: "Mom hates lace, and our dresses are totally lace. Weird!"

"They have this redeeming semi-train-type hemline though." I stand, turning to showcase it.

"And the store had it in all three sizes we needed," says the practical Gina.

"It's settled then—three purple laces for three lovely lasses," I declare with hands on my hips, twisting my hair atop my head for elegance. "Now we just need those purple-dyed matching shoes and we'll be complete," I suggest as all three of us giggle again, form a huddle, and point our toes into the circle.

"I, for one, am going to take this thing off now. I really hate this ugly, flouncy, purply thing." Gina frowns, pulling at the sleeves. I don't blame her. As fashion queen, she knows it is not the style for her. Well, big, puffy sleeves might not be a style for anyone. Parading in front of my big mirrors hasn't changed her opinion one iota either. "But I will endure, and I will even smile" she affirms as she makes a hasty retreat out of my room.

I admire her flash of maturity, letting Mom win this duel gracefully.

Turning towards big sis, I say, "Torr, you look absolutely stunning in yours—regal and ethereal. I must call Tosh with that word. I bet she doesn't know what it means!"

"Do you know what it means, little sister?" she questions me with raised eyebrows and a chuckle.

"Of course. Never doubt my supreme knowledge of unimportant trivia!" I remind her, while sticking my nose in the air and jutting my chin as she, too, heads back to her room, leaving me alone again.

As I again study my reflection in my mirrors, I assess that I look pretty good too, despite the awful colour. I could pass for twenty-one, and I feel pretty and petite—maybe even prepossessing! I'm actually not sure what that means, but it seems just right.

Dad, I wish you could see me. You'd be so proud of me, I think in my mind.

I saw Mom in her gown today. Ho-lee! Mom wasn't just Mom; she made me breathless. She is always coordinated but casual. That dress of sheen and pearls and miles of train makes her young and kind of dramatic—a captivating stranger. A stranger: my mom the stranger. Dad's gone and my mom is still here, but she is a stranger.

I get the chills. My mind goes catapulting in all different directions. I feel out of place—me, the daughter, watching my mom prepare to be married. How out of sync is that? I don't like it.

"What do you think, Dad? Do you approve? Do you understand? Do you feel betrayed? Are we betraying you? Where are you? I wish … I wish we were still simply a nice, normal family. The ways things used to be. Simple. No explaining. I could just be me. No scary days. No scary future. No strangers in my life becoming brothers and stepdad."

Fall 1991

We all have survived the wedding day, Mom being gone on a three-week honeymoon in January, and Mr Man (that's what I call the new man in the house) occasionally being around.

There is no farm and no horse; he didn't want us to move to his place. He said it would be too disruptive for us. Fat chance! He spends most of his time there, though. He says his sons need his help.

We made a surprise trip to visit once, arriving at their house in town while he was at the farm. We brought a full meal to cook, and we gallantly cleaned his messy place, starting in the kitchen.

Oh, was he mad when he got home!

"Don't move anything around in here ever again. Why are you here unannounced? Checking up on me, are you?" he ranted, storming around.

We left the full meal behind and cautiously all piled into our vehicle and left him to his sacred domain.

We've never been back. Mom never goes there any more either. We just live with his strange behaviour whenever he does show up here.

Surprise. I hear his car in the front driveway. I carefully peek out my curtains. My heart sinks as my eyes confirm it's him. Must be at least ten days since he left unannounced, and none of us are expecting him now. What a strange fellow. I wonder if he'll acknowledge me on this visit. I'll be brave and risk a snub.

"Hi there," I say all cheery like as I bound into his view.

He looks at me briefly and then turns and hangs his coat in the front closet, saying nothing.

I try again. "Um, hello?"

Without looking at me this time, he passes me and heads down the hallway, leaving me feeling as if I'm invisible and totally unimportant.

I guess that's the tone of this visit; I should be getting used to it, but it's so creepy! I think he has changed his mind about "always wanting a daughter"!

Oh well, my life is pretty good. I have new friends. They like spending time at our house. We have a trampoline and a hot tub, and Mom enjoys our goofiness. My friends like her.

I've learned to hang out with my friends elsewhere when Mr Man is around.

I'm in grade ten now—high school. Grade nine didn't go well, but I squeaked through. Torr and I ride the city bus together. Another change is coming—Mom's going back to university and completing her master's degree. We'll all be students.

"Mom, I bet you are going to be the nerdy type!" I opine while grabbing an apple out of the fruit basket on the kitchen table and take a big, noisy, juicy bite.

"What do you mean by that, young lady?" she asks with a frown as she turns from unloading groceries.

"You know—you'll complete assignments, do the required reading, study, and get top grades."

"Maybe my good example will rub off on the rest of you," she banters back, and she tosses an orange my way to add to the fruit basket.

I choose to change the subject before pursuing that any

further; already I feel pressure. She hasn't said too much about our plummeting grades. She has tried to get me in to see a grief counsellor, though. For heaven's sake! What next. As if I'd spill my guts to a stranger looking at me with a microscope. I'm sure she's a nice lady and all, but I'll pass for now. I'm doing fine. I'm not all morbid and teary; that's all.

"What does *Mr Man* think about you going back to university?" I ask in a sing-song voice, doing a little hip-hop dance distraction.

"I haven't seen him for a while, as you know," she replies, continuing to pour a bag of flour into the big storage container. "I doubt he cares, Noelle Cheri. I am just making an effort to do something, anything, to make my mind work again."

"Mom, I'm really sorry I said I wished you had died instead of Dad," I blurt out.

"Mrs Mouse," she replies, using Dad's pet name for me and gently cupping my face with her hands, flour and all, "I understand. We're all rather crazy these days. And I'm truly sorry that I've added *Mr Man* to our woes. That family has been friends of your dad and me for over twenty years. Obviously I didn't really know him."

We hug, our tears mingling with choking laughter. Then Mom wipes the flour from my face before we get back to putting groceries away.

Both Torr and I have decided to quit band this year, and Gina never seems to pick up the trumpet either.

Only Torr is still taking piano lessons, though Mom keeps trying to talk her out of it.

"Victoria, you know you need to conserve your energy. You've got to cut something out."

"Cut something out. Hmm, let's see. Like maybe a kidney!" I say as a joke. No one thinks it's funny, though, and they just give me a crushing stare. Under my breath, I add, "Maybe *Mr Man* too." Our house is full of black humour since the tornado hit our family, so why can't anyone see the humour in this? I just don't get this family any more! If Dad were still here, he'd get my humour; he understood me. Now I so often feel alone, like an outsider.

As I attack today's chore list, quickly dusting the main floor, I keep watch out of the windows, not wanting to get surprised by *Mr Man* sneaking in. I don't need his rude silent treatment at the end of the day. Staying out of his path is my only defence—and being first to the hot tub too. So far it looks like he's a no-show. Yahoo.

Torr turns sixteen in a few weeks, and as I come in dripping wet from the hot tub, I catch Torr and Mom in discussion. "Victoria, the Citadel in Edmonton features the play *Sweet Sixteen* next weekend, and I thought it would be fun and special to get tickets, stay in a hotel, and get in some clothes shopping for your special birthday. Interested?"

"Wow, I think I just might be interested, Mom!" teases Torr uncharacteristically. I slowly head to my room, keeping my ears tuned; I'm paying careful attention to everything because it spells future fun for me and Gina too. We'll be sweet sixteen someday as well.

The problem with Torr's birthday, though, is that it signals Christmas is nearby.

Christmas is different now. Mom has to be prodded along through all the steps: Get a tree. Decorate the house. Get gifts. Play Christmas music starting in November. Plan for Christmas guests or Christmas travel. It seems as if she'd like to forget it entirely. Oh well, we'll just keep marching her through the paces, and someday maybe she'll be into it again. I think she just misses Dad and all the used-to-be fun times even more than ever at this time of year.

I miss Dad too. I haven't seen him for almost two years. Wow. Would he know me? I've changed a lot. I'm taller. I'm sassier. I'm … I don't know what I am. I know I want Dad to know me and be proud of me.

Summer 1992

Thank heavens for time away at summer camp again. I am able to pretend my life is normal and just slip back into my old life. It's always amazing how friends you haven't seen for a year are your best friends all over again. And the boys get cuter every year too.

Now on my week home for a break, I decide to inquire. "You're coming as camp nurse this summer, right?" I call to Mom in the back yard.

She turns from cutting her cherished sweet peas, brushes her dark hair out of her eyes, and squints back at me in the bright sunlight. "I'm certainly hoping to. They've asked me for the second week of August and any others I can manage, but I'm thinking of just that one week for this year."

"I always feel safest when you are there, Mom," I say truthfully.

"Thanks for the vote of confidence, little lady." She straightens again, smiles back at me, and rubs her lower back.

"Hey, remember last year, when that young boy got a bat in the face and it split his nose right in half? Blood and gore city, that one!"

"I will never forget that little fellow," she recalls, shaking her head.

"You assigned me to cordon off the kids trying to get a front-row seat to the gore. I'm glad I'm not squeamish like Gina," I say, and I hold the cut flowers for her as she clips more from the long row beautifying the side of the garage in multiple hues.

"You should be a nurse too someday, Noelle-Cheri." She says, not missing a chance to encourage me to think about my future.

"I remember him on the ground, rocking back and forth, eyes wide in terror," I say, avoiding her career nudge. You put pressure on that ghastly wound with some gauze from your magic fanny pouch and calmed him with words, coaching him to breathe slowly through his mouth. It was almost hypnotic watching you, and he bravely did as you asked. But I saw him really relax once you told him he could talk with his parents once you got to the hospital. Those were magic words for him."

Parents are so important, I think to myself as I head inside to put the flowers in a vase. *I am glad I at least have Mom.*

"Hey, Gina, have you heard if Maggie can join us for our week out at Fairmont?" I ask when I find her in her room organizing her stuff for camp.

"She is actually staying with her sister in Edmonton, so will be able to join us," Gina answers. I just found out last night."

"It will be nice to see her again."

After supper, Gina broaches a conversation sure to raise the stress in our family. She's determined to head off to private school. I catch some of the conversation.

"Gina, you're too young to be so far from home for such an extended period of time, and so unnecessarily so. I believe your family is more essential than any special school you might hear of."

"Mom, I just think it would be good for me," she says, starting to clear the dishes. "Westpark Junior High doesn't do it for me. You know that. You took me out for a few weeks and homeschooled me. They don't want me back either."

"That doesn't matter." Mom sounds riled up. "Whether they want you or not, they have to take you. I'll see to that."

"It's no use, Mom. I don't want to go back. I want to go to Caronport. They take grade niners."

"How do you know that?" Mom queries, sounding suspicious, and she tosses the tea towel in the sink like an unwanted rotten potato. "Besides," she says more calmly, "you'll miss your friends."

I guess Mom thinks she'll hit a home run with that comment, but I don't think so. And I'm right again. It doesn't even slow Gina down. I know Gina's determined to make a change. She must be braver than me. The confines of home sometimes drive me crazy, but leaving and going far away all alone scares the you-know-what out of me.

After a tense empty moment, Mom states quietly, "Gina, Victoria is leaving this fall for College in Saskatchewan; I don't want you to go too. It feels strange for her to be going, but you have no reason to go yet. Please be reasonable."

"Mom, I've thought about this a lot, and I think it's what I need. Please think about that. You'll still have N. C. at home," Gina argues back.

"That's not the point, Gina," Mom says, plopping down hard on a kitchen chair, wiping her wet hands roughly and sounding exasperated. "You have at least four more years to have and enjoy your home and family before heading out into the big world. Take advantage of that, honey." Mom is passionate about her belief in the plusses of family life.

"I want to go, Mom. I want to go to Caronport High School. I want to start over. I know this is best." Gina sounds so mature and convincing. I marvel at her confidence and strong stance. I wonder if she just wants to get away from the landmine our home has become with Mr Man coming and going.

The discussion ended, and the weeks have gone by. I'm not sure where everything sits at the moment. I think Gina has phoned for the application package, but she'll need Mom to sign her approval. She'll probably get it. She gets everything she wants. Mom's no match.

Tomorrow we're supposed to head to our timeshare in beautiful British Columbia for our family holiday. It was fun last year. The new brothers came, and we all had a great holiday.

This year they aren't coming because they're working, but it will still be fun, I hope, even with Mr Man and his moods.

As I pass through the kitchen with clean clothes to pack in the motor home, I see Mom hunched over a kitchen chair and hissing through her teeth.

"What's up, Mom?"

"That was him on the phone. Says he can't make it after all. Wants to get some things done on the farm." I hear anger in her voice.

"Who? Mr Man?" I ask incredulously. The motor home is packed, and all arrangements have been made. Now this bit of news. Who does he think he is? No reason given—just a rude, inconsiderate "Not coming."

Without reprimanding me for my sassy "Mr Man," Mom nods as her shoulders slump, and I stand with my armload of clothes, seething at the news.

Mom's vacuuming. She does that a lot. We've come to recognize it as anger management.

Now she's summoning us all together.

"Guys, I think we should still go as planned. I can manage the motor home myself, and you can help with some things. We'll take our time getting there. There's no rush. Are you game?"

It's an easy and unanimous decision. So we hit the road, five women and a motor home. I'll even designate Gina and Maggie as women.

Well, Mr Man, you can't ruin our lives all the time, I think gleefully.

Borneo has to stay home. The resort doesn't allow pets. He'll manage. He's street-smart, and we set out enough food for the entire neighbourhood of cats. Plus we alerted our next-door friend, and she's so good to us. She'll keep a good lookout for Borneo.

I feel fun bubbling up inside. This will be a new adventure. Mom sounds strong and upbeat, and there's a warm sun with nary a puffy cloud in sight. What could possibly go wrong?

I remember going to Fairmont in my past life with Dad too. We didn't have a timeshare then but stayed at the resort hotel. Being the natural fish that I am, I loved the hours in the pool. Dad never tired of diving competitions or seeing who could swim the farthest underwater. Of course, he always won. *Maybe I could beat him now*, I imagine. We would line up chest deep in that pool and swim underwater through everyone's spreadeagle legs too. Even Mom did it. That was if we could keep from falling over laughing. Those were fun times. Dad was fun. Mom was happy. We were happy. Now we're all … different.

"Hey, Mom, you haven't even pulled over to nap yet!" I yell down from the queen-size over-cab bed I lie snuggled in, reading my mystery novel.

"Funny girl," Mom answers good-humouredly, acknowledging her penchant for getting sleepy in vehicles.

I always preferred Dad's driving, because I knew he wouldn't fall asleep, but now we don't have any choice. Torr certainly isn't ready for driving the big rig.

I'm old enough to be driving, and I finally have my learner's permit, but I just don't want that real licence to drive. Not yet. I don't know what's holding me back. Maybe Dad's accident messes up my interest in learning to drive. Maybe it's that little accident I experienced with Flora this year. The lady who rammed us struck my door, the passenger side. I thought I was a goner. Kind of shook me up. It was terrifying watching it come straight for me, the thud and crunching, sounds and wondering what would happen to me. I never told Mom about it for fear she'd ban all outings with Flora.

I wonder what Dad thought as he realized he couldn't avoid hitting the train … Did his life pass before his eyes like the books say? Did he think of us and wish he could say goodbye? I hope he didn't feel anything. I always dream that the train he hit was like a Nerf toy, all soft and cushy.

Looking out the window at the large, lush grain fields rolling by, my thoughts swing back to my holiday ahead, and I realize we're almost to Cochrane already.

"Girls, shall we take the scenic route or head on to the faster Trans-Canada Highway?" Mom asks.

"Scenic!" we chime, and we all squeeze onto the over-cab bunk for a watchtower advantage.

Mom obligingly turns off on Highway 1A. Narrow, winding, and wooded on both sides, it adds to the fun of the ride in the back of the motorhome.

Mom sees a sign for a campground and decides she's had enough driving for the day. Setting up camp will be fun. I'm glad we decided to head out without Mr Man; I'm sure we can do this.

The road's getting rough, and we're rapidly climbing. We're going slower and slower, and things are completely quiet. We haven't seen any camping sites or check-in building … it's strange.

"Girls, get down off the bunk," Mom says with urgency.

Just then a tree scrapes noisily along the right side of our unit. We are on a ridge looking down a long, cavernous way, and the single-lane trail feels too narrow for our rig. We can't turn around, and I don't think Mom would try to back all the way down, so I just hope and pray the road widens out again and we make it to safety.

Slowly we progress, Mom silent and white-knuckled on the steering wheel, and us girls bug-eyed in terror.

Finally, after what seems a lonely eternity, we are back down in a meadow area and heading for the exit. Everyone heaves a sigh of relief.

"I think we'll just continue on to Canmore" is Mom's facetiously calm assessment. I'm certainly wide awake! "There must be an open site at that campground this time of day; at least it will still be daylight."

We all nod in relieved agreement and try to relax now that we have missed falling to our death in that canyon.

"I don't think Dad would have made this mistake," I grumble to myself. I always felt safe when he was driving.

Safe, I think.

Safe.

Dad, how come you didn't see that train coming? I scream in my mind. One mistake and *bam*, no more Dad. No more family.

I hear his confident promise. "We'll always be family, Ms Mouse."

Later, settled in the new campground, we strike out, following Spring Creek Trail for a long, long way.

We skip stones in the creek, and I feel Dad beside me, coaching me as he did so many times before, and I find the perfect thin, round stone.

I hear his approval. "That's the one, N. C."

"Mine definitely went the farthest and bounced the most times," I declare.

"Not a chance," says Gina. "Mine even bounded up on the other shore!"

"As if!" I ridicule. "I didn't see it."

Peacemaker Torr intervenes with "Let's see if we can wade across to the other side. It looks shallow enough."

"It also looks swift and rocky," I add.

Stepping in bravely, Gina declares it to be lovely.

Foolishly believing her, I start in as well, only to shriek, "It's frigid!" while hopping about on the foot-punishing stones. I quickly abandon the venture and watch as my sisters and Maggie rush across and exit the other bank.

Laughing, I congratulate them and remind them, "Now you have to repeat the feat to make it back here before the bears get you!"

My comment is motivation enough to bring them back my way tout de suite.

I always dread the "Let's go for a little hike" suggestion, but as we return to our site, I realize it was fun. Memories of Dad fill my heart, but they make it hurt too.

"Tomorrow we'll easily make it to Fairmont Hot Springs," Mom says, though our rig might complain on some of those mountain climbs.

For no reason I can see, we all get the giggles.

We sleep well and enjoy a camping breakfast of pancakes the next morning.

This trip is fun already, and I will try to be positive about the planned stop at famed Lake Louise.

Mom and Dad always liked to take us there and do the tea house hike. I was always the first to the top, and I liked the halfway rest at the little lake on the trail up. Dad would plunge into the cold waters and goad us to follow. *I wonder if we'll do that today*, I think with a tight feeling in my chest. Why did I always complain about it? *Maybe Dad will speak to me there today*, I think hopefully.

I'm really glad Mr Man isn't with us.

Today, we don't go in the halfway lake, but we stand quietly together, catching our breath and chugging from our water bottles, as fellow hikers pass by.

"Mom, are you going to lead us in for a cool-off dip?" I inquire, not sure whether I want her to.

"No. I think not. Only your dad could do that," she wisely returns with a small grin and sad eyes.

Finally we head on up the mountain, less enthusiastically.

I always feel like royalty ordering tea and goodies when we get to the top. What a view, and what crazy chipmunks and crazy tourists There is a guy doing magic tricks while balanced on the rocks in the creek at the top of the waterfall. We caught glimpses of his daring silhouetted feat while we climbed the last excruciating hundred feet of rock stairs. *OK, Mom, I guess it's all right that you made me come here against my will*, I think.

There are people here from all over the world, and I hear lots of different languages. I like that. It's a reminder the world is much bigger than I usually think about—a reminder there are places and things I haven't seen or done.

This time it is also a reminder we're here without Dad. I feel a familiar but unwanted tightness in my chest.

Our week at the Villa starts out fine. Its familiar, spacious luxury, wrapped in mountain vistas, makes me light-hearted, and a TV in every room makes me delirious; this is my kind of setting. All four of us girls nest in the en suite second bedroom that has its own compact kitchen and private entrance. Mom is welcome to the palatial master bedroom as long as we girls can intrude and overtake the big spa tub whenever we want. That is my rule, anyway.

"Hey, Mom, are the Gradys going to be staying over tonight?" I ask as I see her starting preparations for a barbecue, and I know our family friends from Rocky Mountain House are arriving soon. "Sandy and Helene are going to be with them, right?"

"Yes, they are staying over, and no, the kids aren't coming this time."

"So I'm stuck with just siblings and Maggie for the whole week?" I complain with hands on my hips and a snarl in my voice. "When did you find that out?" I ask accusingly.

"I guess a week ago. Sorry; I thought I told you," she says, looking up from making hamburger patties. "I know you guys have had so much fun in the past, but things happen, Noelle Cheri, and plans change."

"That's for sure. When is something good going to happen though?" I storm on and turn to leave in a huff.

"Noelle-Cheri, you can help me prepare the barbecue," she says in her disciplinary voice, giving a harsh look to settle the point.

Could be worse, I guess, I think as my quick flare of steam goes out of me.

Shortly after dinner, it does get worse. While deciding what we all plan to do the next day, there is a knock on the door, and there is Mr Man!

Well, surprise and hellfire a-coming down.

He claims he changed his mind and caught a Greyhound bus to

come join us after all. He is cranky from the long ride cramped in the bus, which challenged his long limbs, and the long walk from the bus station to the villa in the lingering heat of the early evening. Somehow or other, these problems are our fault.

Everyone is surprised to see him, and I think Mom looks a little embarrassed in front of our friends after explaining why he wasn't with us and then having him appear from out of nowhere.

The mood is different now. We're all on edge. Mom will be trying to keep him happy and keep everything smooth. Our friends are gracious and carry on as before. Maybe only I am aware of the change that has just occurred. I'm not very hopeful of any more fun happening this week. Oh well, I've got a good book along. I'll just stay out of his way best I can.

As I'm lounging after supper on the deck with my eyes closed, my mind wanders and I review my situation.

When this week is over, it's grade eleven for me, and Lindsay Thurber Composite High School will, I hope, be old hat for me—no surprises. With Torr gone, I will ride the city bus alone and defy the gang girls alone, but I feel confident.

I'm not sure how things are going for Gina. In July, Mom relented and agreed to her request for private school. Then, just before we left for Fairmont, Gina changed her mind and wanted to stay home for schooling again this year. I see that row afresh in my mind:

"Gina, you plotted and badgered and reasoned this into being. Your admission stuff is all complete, and now it's a done deal. *You are not changing your mind now.* We've all been through too much turmoil with this to just recant." Mom stormed on and on. "I quit fighting that wind of change and agreed to support your decision despite how I felt about such things. Now I have to make you follow through on it, and I don't even believe in it. This is so crazy." She flung her hands in the air.

"If you make me go, I'll commit suicide," Gina threatened.

Ho-leeee! That sounded like a line I'd come up with, but not

Gina. Life can get so complex so quickly. I wondered how Mom would deal with that scary threat.

Very slowly and very quietly, Mom continued. "You will go, and you will not commit suicide. This discussion is over." She stood, shaking.

I wondered if my family would totally fall apart. I wondered if Gina really meant her threat. I wondered if there was anything I could say to lighten the situation. I just wanted to get away from it all.

I wanted to hear Dad say, "We will always be a family, Ms Mouse."

There hasn't been any further discussion that I know of, and so far, no more threats of suicide. Thank you, God. I'm pretty confident Gina would never do anything so crazy, but I know she is desperate for some change in our family. I guess we all are.

September 1992

I think I'll go on the road trip planned for next week, taking Torr to Millar College and then Gina on to Caronport just a couple of hours further east, near Moose Jaw. I don't think Mr Man is going, so that's sweet by me.

I hope Gina's surgery is going well. Mom has finally agreed to the tonsillectomy Gina needs for her continuous throat infections, despite it meaning she'll miss the first week of school. Today is the day. Glad it's not me!

Gina faints just talking about blood and gore, so I'm not sure how she'll do with being gored herself. It's an ugly, dangerous surgery, according to Mom, and that cute little paediatric ward isn't really going to soften the blow one iota.

I hear Mom talking to Grandma on the phone. "I'm heading

back up to the hospital. Gina should be coming out of recovery soon".

I guess I'll soon know how little sister is doing.

I rather like blood and gore, but I say, "Mom, I'm going to stay and read my book. You can tell me all about Gina when you get back."

As it turns out, the story is rather interesting. Nurses had trouble getting a blood pressure reading with the machine. Perhaps this was because of the anaesthetic and the effects of medications, as Mom explained. Besides, low pressure is the bane of her family. Gina was alert, so Mom concluded the pressure was adequate, even though it was too low to register. There was no panic from this old veteran nurse. *Yeah, Mom! You should have been an army sergeant major or something like that.*

Gina has been in hospital two nights and will be discharged this morning. We'll pick her up and head for Saskatchewan via one night in Medicine Hat. You've got to be tough in this family.

"Gina you look more dead than alive," I say, greeting her cheerily as she climbs into the motorhome and quickly lies down on the bed. She remains unmoving and only risks casting her eyes my direction.

My words are truth too. How can she travel and head off to school all by herself in such condition—as white as a sheet and as weak as a kitten. She swallows with exaggerated throat movement, obviously in a lot of pain, and she dabs her mouth, the tissue showing bloody saliva. This doesn't look good. She doesn't answer but gives me a doleful look. I feel sorry for her being in pain and having to leave home for school now that she doesn't want to go any more.

At least travel with the motor home gives her a couple more days lying around, and she has her own private nurse, Mom, along. I'll just trust in that and ignore that nasty saliva.

It's a bright, sunny day for driving, and again we're taking the scenic route, only going east not west this time. More adventure is coming our way, I guess.

Driving through the Badlands' gorges sounded like a great idea yesterday. Today, the reality of it with the motor home doesn't seem as good an idea.

I don't think Gina cares; she's just moaning and surviving.

Torr just exudes excitement at being on her way to college and a new adventure, though I know new things always stress her out.

The night's darkness, now upon us, is not a friend, but I visualize Dad in the driver's seat. I indulge myself with the feeling that he's with us for this time of big change in our lives, even if the fantasy only lasts for moments.

I am refreshed now after a night with our friends in Medicine Hat—a good night—and a hearty breakfast for everyone but Gina. Today we're heading on to Millar. Thankfully, Gina is doing better at last. There is no more bloody saliva, and she even ate a little mushy cereal at breakfast. She still looks awfully pale though. There's no more moaning; that's a good sign.

I think she's missing Borneo already too. We all love him, but Gina is his favourite now that Dad is gone. Too bad you can't take a pet to Caronport. That would help her a lot.

Travel today is uneventful, and Gina manages to sit up most of the day.

As we near Millar, Torr seems to retreat and have little to say. Her enthusiasm seems to have dwindled, and I suspect she'd like to change her mind too and go back home. She wisely doesn't verbalize it. I hate to think what Mom would have to say.

Settling Torr into her room and meeting her roommate is far from boring. We all like interior decorating and set about creating a homey nest.

I sense Torr is feeling better about her survival here, and she knows some of the girls in her hallway. They are from summer camp, and that's why she chose Millar. Plus Max, the camp director, is the phys-ed instructor here. She'll do well, I know, but it feels funny to have big sister actually leave home. Now I'm the big sister. Except little sister will be gone too, so that leaves me alone. Change! Change! Life is always changing.

Tomorrow we'll be on to Caronport to get Gina settled into dorm there.

Thankfully, I'm privy to their compromise discussion just before bed.

"Gina," Mom says, sitting on a chair by her, settled into the bottom bunk of a guest room, and offering another icy Popsicle and bowl of Jell-O, "I have a suggestion. A compromise. I hope you can agree to it."

I see hope in Mom's expression and wariness in Gina's eyes as she tilts her face as if asking a silent question.

"What suggestion?" Gina croaks as she bites the green Popsicle hungrily.

I hold my breath in anticipation.

"I need you to commit to attending here for this first semester." I'm still holding my breath, wondering how this is a compromise. "But," she continues, "you can come back home for second semester." Her words rush out.

"Thanks, Mom," is the croaky response, which is accompanied by a look of relief followed by a long hug.

I guess our family survived another crisis and we're still intact. Relationships are fragile things. Life is fragile.

I'm glad I'm just living at home and going to my same school and hanging with my same friends and enjoying the hot tub and having no one to share the phone with. This is going to be a very good year. I can feel it.

However, next morning before we get on the road, Torr throws a curve; looks like another relationship is being added to our mix. There goes my good year, I fear.

"Mom, do you think it'd be OK for Fanny to use my room while I'm away? She's so mature and helpful and has no place to stay. She could use my car and drive N. C. to school like I did. In all the packing and such, I forgot to mention it till now. Sorry."

"Torr, what is her situation anyway?" Mom asks, wanting more details, I assume.

"Well, I'm not sure of all the details, but she has no family to live with. You remember her from our youth group, right?"

"Yes, of course I remember her, but I didn't know she was in such dire straits. Where is she staying now?"

"I don't know the family, but it sounds like they need more space for their own family now," Torr explains.

Mom's a sucker for the underdog, so it's a given she'll say yes. No one seems to be asking my opinion. Torr really likes Fanny, but I think she's bossy, manipulative, self-righteous, and just plain boring. She's just using Torr, and now she'll use my mom. I think Fanny is a true orphan even though her parents are alive. That they've abandoned their kids is my take on the whole affair.

I'm not a true orphan. I still have my mom, and she tries to be what we need in this crazy tornado world we find ourselves in. I don't think she'll have much luck with Fanny.

Winter 1992

It's been a few months, and just as I predicted, Mom agreed to Torr's request to take in orphan Fanny. I'm going to watch this chick like a hawk. She'd better not expect to borrow my things, or start preaching to my friends, or knock my home all upside down. I'd like a little continuity for a while—and what about my chance to be the big shot for once? The big sister! And the only daughter for a while too. Now I've got competition again. I hope Mom is not snowed by this chick and impressed with her so-called maturity.

The weeks are passing, and Torr sounds really happy on the phone and tells me she is loving college life. I'm doing all right on the home front despite "Perfect Fanny" being on the scene. Mom seems to love her studies and hates her job at the walk-in clinic, enduring the obsessive-compulsive doctor. I bet I could figure him out. Maybe I'll be a psychiatrist when I grow up. That sounds a tad scary. I don't want to grow up. It looks too unpredictable.

Dad, I wish you were here to talk with.

I'm so glad Gina will soon be home from Caronport. She'll bring some balance to this house of women. I say "women" because Mr Man is usually absent and pretty much invisible even when here. He ignores us and pretends we're not present. He's like having a ghost in our home—a malevolent, hostile ghost—but I can usually survive unscathed. Fanny is another matter.

"Fanny!" I call. "Oh, there you are. Have you seen my brown leather bomber jacket?" I ask knowingly.

I can tell she goes in my room when I'm not here. She does indeed borrow my things without asking. Hey, I've done that to my sisters—and with poor results too. But she's not my sister. She's not my friend. She's just a thorn in the flesh.

"N. C., I think I saw it on the sofa downstairs," she responds sweetly and innocently, but I'm not fooled.

I don't think Mom is fooled by her any more either.

Finding Fanny doing a messy painting project on our dining room table one day, Mom requested with patience, "Fanny, I'd like you to confine projects like these to the kitchen table—a much easier place to clean up after." Knowing my mom, I suspected she had counted to at least ten before speaking when she walked in on that mess.

Batting big blue eyes of innocence and shock, Fanny stood her ground, saying, "But I need this bigger surface. The round kitchen table just doesn't work that well."

"Sorry about that, Fanny, but I can't afford damage to the dining table or the carpet, so limit these types of projects to the kitchen," Mom insisted.

Fanny turned on the tears and tried a guilt tactic with "Well, I'll just have to find a space at school or a friend's house, I guess."

"Sounds good, Fanny. Thanks for understanding" was Mom's facetious reply, which she delivered with a straight face. I almost laughed out loud, pretty sure Fanny was not understanding one iota.

I think the constant inconsiderate phone usage is the biggest issue so far though. The three of us have gathered tonight for that discussion.

"Thanks, girls, for setting time aside for a discussion," Mom starts. "We need to find a solution to the phone usage."

"What problem is that?" asks Fanny, smiling and seemingly clueless, but I notice her begin tapping her pen on her notebook.

"Well, speaking for myself only, I am often needing to make a call in the evening, and you are using the phone. Your calls are often really long, up to an hour even. And people are telling me they can't get through in the evening. My parents in particular aren't comfortable in just leaving messages. We've missed many chances for phone visits from Victoria and Gina, as they can't get through either"

"This is a total surprise to me," stammers Fanny, puffing herself up and sitting higher in her chair. I hardly ever use the phone or make long calls," she says, pleading her innocence, and I see her begin to bat her eyes and look deeply wounded, reminding me of my friend's golden lab.

"I know this must seem a surprise to you, Fanny, but I need to let you know this is a problem," Mom continues reasonably. "I can show you the phone bills if that will help you." I stay out of the discussion, enjoying the observer role this time.

"My family and friends are counting on me," Fanny says, changing tack. "They need me."

Ah, bring out the guilt, Fanny, I think to myself. *That's your trademark.*

"The thing is, Fanny, we all have family and friends *counting on us.* There are three of us here, and soon Gina as well, making at least four. I'm suggesting you choose a night for your long calls or a nightly time block so we each know when the phone is available. Personally, I think we should get a separate line put in for you. I haven't checked what that would cost you, though."

"You just don't understand me," Fanny voices while standing abruptly, and she leaves crying big tears. I almost feel sorry for her, but I then remember her telling me about how she always gets her way with teachers or other persons of authority by using these tactics.

I wonder if Mom's discussion with her even made a dent in Fanny's armour. I see no signs of us getting another phone line yet.

Another thoughtless Fanny assumption is on the horizon.

Fanny plans to use Torr's car over Christmas to drive her and her sister all the way to Saskatchewan to visit her grandparents. Mom just found out yesterday.

"What's this about a trip to Saskatchewan, Fanny?" Mom queries.

"Oh, I always go to my grandparents' at Christmas," explains Fanny with wide, innocent eyes, lashes aflutter. She turns abruptly, as if to hurry on her busy way to save the world.

"That's nice. That's great. How are you getting there?" Mom persists.

Turning back towards Mom, Fanny says innocently, "I'll take the Honda and pick up my sister, and we'll meet my two cousins in Calgary and head on to Saskatchewan, where my grandparents live. They're so excited about the trip, and my grandparents are counting on me to make it all happen like every other year."

I hold my breath as I absorb this audacity. Mom is a giver but is not as good about things being taken from her carte blanche. This on top of all the other shenanigans the last few months! Torr's simple request of giving a home to the homeless is creating a lot of stress in our home.

"Fanny, did you even think it might be wise to ask if you could borrow the car over the holidays?" Mom asks.

"But I use the car all the time. I just assumed I could have it over Christmas," reasons Fanny, her eyes tearing up.

Mom looks stunned by this assumption and remains speechless for a bit.

I had marvelled at her generosity in the first place when she let Fanny use our second car for all her commitments: school, work, youth functions, and her scattered family visits. She was only required to buy her own gas. She did chauffeur me to school sometimes, but only if I was desperate. I preferred to ride the bus. I thought maybe I should get my driver's licence and reverse the roles here.

"Taking the car on a long road trip, in winter, and out of province and with passengers, is quite a different matter," Mom counters. "Plus Victoria will be home to use it, and most importantly, you never even asked. Making all these plans and not consulting the owner is presumptuous and staggering to me."

Now the big tears fall in earnest.

"I have to have the car. Everyone is counting on me. Our Christmas will be ruined." Fanny sniffs through her tears.

What is Mom going to do about this heavy responsibility? I wonder. *She is caught between a rock and a hard place.*

"Fanny, we'll talk about this again tonight. I need time to think this through," cautions Mom.

Phew, a reprieve. Time to cool down and regroup. I hope Mom plays hardball and doesn't weaken just because of tears and the "guilting" ploy about Christmas and others counting on her. If that were me, Mom would make me pay the price for making such stupid choices. She'd say it was a good lesson in maturing and being responsible, learning courtesy, etc. I can't wait to see the outcome of this latest conflict.

The hours have dragged by while I've been waiting to see Mom's decision.

"What are you going to do about the car, Mom?" I venture after school and just before Fanny is due home from her office cleaning job.

Mom shrugs, shakes her head slowly, and presses her lips together, looking disgusted and tired. She looks as if she might need to start vacuuming! Sighing, she admits, "I don't know. I really don't know. I just can't believe this latest stunt. But I feel bad for all the others concerned. Ruining their Christmas feels rather heavy, and we can do fine with one car. More importantly, I have to come up with a solution to the overall problem for sure. What would you suggest, my wise girl?"

"Mom, just think of what you'd do if one of us were so thoughtless or acted as if we were so entitled."

"Ah, there's a reason I call you wise, Noelle-Cheri!" She hugs me, with bright eyes and a big smile.

I feel hope that Mom will be hard on Fanny. I hope she pulls the car out from under Fanny's plans. But at least it looks like something will be done in the near future.

As it turns out, I was totally right in my observation and expectation of the results. I catch a bit of their discussion later that evening.

"Fanny, I am going to let you have the car over Christmas for all your plans, but when you get back, we are going to sit down and rework some boundaries. I am not at all comfortable with what has just occurred here. We need to sit down and discuss expectations on both sides." Mom firmly states. I think I catch a winning smirk on Fanny's face, and I don't hang around for any more discussion. Maybe this is a win-win. It is at least a compromise, but one with a promise of future change.

One good thing about all this is that Fanny is gone for the next ten days and we will just be family. Yeah!

Torr and Gina get home tomorrow.

I'm excited.

I'm ecstatic.

I'm delirious.

This will be a great Christmas. Gina won't have the usual tonsillitis, because her tonsils have been yanked out. Torr will be full of stories from college, and I'm full of stories about Miss Perfect Fanny. Mom is off work and done with courses for a couple of weeks, so we'll just party, dude.

The ceiling-high Christmas tree smells delightful and woodsy, and I'm impressed with my decorating talents; the tree is shining spectacularly in glittering silver, with red bows for accent, and of course our trusty heritage angel is just squeezing in at the top. Mom even put up a few outdoor lights this year, and the humongous trees out front are loaded with snow. Beauty is everywhere. It even seems peaceful. What more could I want?

I want Dad. Wouldn't that be a great Christmas gift? We'd go chop down our own fresh evergreen. He'd put up a zillion outdoor lights. There'd be tons of gifts under the tree from our gift-giver, and goofy, misleading gift-wrapping surprises and gift tags with hints of the contents and the giver. I'm good at guessing too! I'd get to hear his strong voice singing heartily on Christmas Eve. And we'd still go pull him out of bed early on Christmas morning and stick a Santa hat on him.

It was a great Christmas. I sang a solo at the Christmas Eve service. Mom cried. She always cries at church, though, since Dad died, so maybe it wasn't my singing that moved her.

We had lots of family in and out over the holidays, including about thirty folks on Boxing Day, our annual family bowling day. It's a tradition. I love watching everyone bowl. Grandma and Grandpa get great scores because they're in a senior league. They're old pros. The under-fivers get great scores because their slower-than-molasses balls seem to do amazing feats. I don't score well at all, but it doesn't matter one bit. It's all fun and snacks and laughter and tradition.

Tradition! That's like normal. That's like "you can count on it". That's like you know what to expect. I like it.

We have a new tradition too. We place an evergreen arrangement with a centre candle, to honour Dad in our lives—especially at Christmastime. This year it is on the dining room table.

January 1993

I waltz into Torr's bedroom and lie across her bed on my stomach, looking up at her, and ask brightly to mask my upcoming loss, "Torr, are you heading back to college tomorrow?"

"I'm afraid so, N. C.," she responds as she looks up from her packing. "This has been a great break, but I'm excited to head back. I really am enjoying the time there." She gives the suitcase zip a tug and smiles broadly.

I know she's taking voice lessons and loving the big choir experience and sports opportunities too. Her stories of dorm life sound pretty crazy, and sneaking trips off campus in the middle of the night sounds like something I would do, not Torr. Maybe growing up won't be too dull after all.

"I'll miss you, Torr," I say quietly, and I move off her bed to plop onto her desk chair. "I'm glad you're enjoying your new life; honestly, I am." I give myself a full spin in the desk chair to seem light-hearted.

"N. C., you sound sad. Are you OK?" Torr asks, and she brings my spinning chair to a full stop.

"Sure," I quickly respond. Why wouldn't I be?" I force a smile and lift my chin as if questioning her assessment.

"You just go ahead and enjoy your majestic, mysterious, fun years at college," I say in mock seriousness, making a sweeping gesture with my hand. "I'll be joining you soon enough, you know. I'm ready, even now, to accept the challenge of initiation into adulthood." I say this with my usual bravado to reassure big sis and give her an impromptu reassuring hug to boot.

"I'll call often, N. C.," she promises with firm eyes upon me as we separate. I know she will. I can count on her.

"Come join me in the hot tub, Torr; it's our last night together for a while," I say breezily, and I head off to my room before tears betray me.

Getting back into school routine again, I realize I better just tackle this semester and try to pass grade eleven. At least Gina is back home, spunky and feisty as always, so I'm guessing Miss Perfect Fanny will be knocked down a peg or two even if Mom caves.

I'm a middle child, and that means I play the peacekeeping role, avoid confrontation, and seethe inwardly rather than face my nemesis. Gina has a different technique.

"Watch her and weep," I always say. This time I say, "Watch her and cheer."

If Fanny crosses the sacred threshold of Gina's room, I know it won't happen a second time. If Fanny tries batting big blue eyes of innocence, Gina will just scoff. If there is progression to the weeping and "poor me" strategy, Gina will outright laugh at her blatant manipulation.

Things are definitely changing around here; I can feel it. I think Fanny is sensing it too. I wasn't privy to the post-Christmas talk she had with Mom, but I've heard her talking with her super perfect friends at school about getting a live-in babysitting job somewhere. It's time to find some new family to domineer and dazzle, I suspect.

"Mom, is Fanny moving out?" I probe after supper one evening.

I knew Fanny was at the medical clinic, doing her job of office cleaning. It's nearly the end of February, but I'm still optimistic she is going to move on and take her efficiency elsewhere. I plan to be subtle with my fact-finding mission, but it sounds awfully blunt, and maybe too hopeful.

"She hasn't said anything to me about moving. I think our talks went well, and she's respecting the boundaries we discussed. Have you heard something?"

"No, nothing really." I turn away, carrying dishes to the sink. "It's just a feeling plus her talk of getting a different job."

Mom looks thoughtful and speaks carefully as she scrapes left over lasagne into a fridge container. "I think she needs to control us all to feel safe. It's not working, of course, so you may be right. Maybe she is thinking of moving on." Mom sounds a little sad and wistful.

"You've been good to her, Mom," I heartily add.

"Maybe someone else can get through to her," Mom says with a small smile and a sigh. "Let's just wait and see what develops."

It's two days since my talk with Mom about Fanny leaving.

As I get off the bus, I can see Fanny loading things into the Honda in our front driveway.

I'm walking faster and faster, trying not to look unusual but not wanting to miss anything that's happening. Thank heavens I didn't go to the mall after school with Flora.

"Hey Fanny, what's up?" I ask a little breathlessly as I come up the driveway.

"Hi, N. C. I'm moving. I got a job with the Walker family, and they want me to live in with them."

I wondered if she had told my mom, but I didn't want to find out that she hadn't.

"Have you got everything packed already?" I politely inquire.

"I'll have to come back for one more load, probably after I finish at the medical clinic—my last night."

"So your new job starts tomorrow?" I press.

"That's right. They're so pleased to have me. It will make Mrs Walker's life so much simpler to have me right there for whenever she needs to be at the office. And I just love those two sweeties of hers.

It's a total answer to prayer." She prattles on while stuffing boxes and bags in the boot of our car.

Yes, you can go organize those poor folks, I think, *and leave us alone. Go ahead and save the world. Go where you're admired and held on a pedestal. Go heed the call to martyrdom. Go mother those two sweeties deserted by their own mother. Go, Go. Go. You have my blessing. Someday you might even realize what you are throwing away by leaving our home.*

I feel so lucky to have my home, my sisters, my mom, my family. I could be adrift like Fanny, trying to create a home, control a family, and find significance.

I just need a dad and haven't even tried to create one, because no one could replace him. The familiar feeling churns my gut. "I just need you, Dad," I say under my breath as I watch this person determinedly choose to walk out of our lives.

"Goodbye, Fanny, and good luck," I throw back to her sincerely as I escape to my room.

When Mom gets home from work, I'll have to inform her of the news. I'm sure she has no idea; this is just Fanny's way of jerking us around. I hope she doesn't plan to keep the car. Surely she has her claws on a better one at the Walker household. I realize I had better check the chores list and do my part before heading to the hot tub for my stress-busting soak.

Spring 1993

It's been blissful around here with Fanny gone. Gina and I rarely tangle these days. Maybe we're maturing. Maybe we're subconsciously grateful for what we have. Maybe she's changed since going away to Caronport those few months. She's certainly consumed with her friends and school sports. I can't imagine enjoying sweaty basketball or wimpy badminton or ridiculous track and field events. Now, the trampoline is OK, except for my penchant to continually sprain my ankle on it. And after all, swimming is my gift. Even synchronized is great. I'm currently getting ready for my Bronze Cross.

Tonight is slow pitch—the city church league.

Per usual, we're early.

I see Grandma and Grandpa are just driving up. The weather is cool and windy, but they've parked at an angle to watch from inside their car. I give a wave and head to the pitcher's mound for a couple of warm-up pitches.

As everyone takes their places, I notice Mr Man park nearby. This is one thing he seems to enjoy, and he sometimes joins us, always without notice. He's a team asset, though, when he does show up—a heavy hitter!

I skilfully put the first batter out and walk the second. I am feeling a bit cocky. Maybe Mr Man will notice and say, "well done", or at least say hello. He's sure a strange dude.

Maybe I was daydreaming too much. The next thing I know, I'm lying flat on my back looking up at the grey sky, and pain consumes me. I don't remember even throwing the pitch or the batter slugging it my way.

I hear shouting and try to focus on the numerous faces peering down at me.

"Are you OK?" seems to be the muffled question I hear from the blurry faces. I'm sure I see Dad smiling down at me fleetingly. I want to hold that image.

Nurse, Mother Bear, insists no one move me or help me up.

Eventually I manage on my own, and Mom carts me off to the Red Deer General ER; it's just minutes away, but it seems to take us forever to get there. My eyes are swollen almost shut, with just room for tears to leak out. I wish the pain would leak out!

The others stay to finish the game. *Maybe Mr Man is pitching in my stead*, I think.

As we take our seat in the waiting room, Mom tells me, "It might be a long wait, Nichole-Cheri, but I want you assessed properly."

Her prediction is right; it's a really long wait in the ER!

I hear a siren screaming its way for help nearby, and suddenly the room is filled with many voices and people bustling in, crying and yelling. It feels like the night the RCMP came to our house. I want it to all go away.

"I want to go home, Mom," I plead.

"I know, honey, but you should be seen first. You've had quite the blunt trauma," she reasons with me.

I try to distract myself by chatting with a little girl beside me who is sitting on her dad's knee and sucking her thumb. All this commotion must be scary for her too. My funny facial appearance doesn't seem to bother her. I draw a face on my thumb and pointer finger, all scrunched up, with a pen from Mom's purse. Remembering what Dad taught me, I make talking sounds, moving my thumb like a lower jaw. She is a good audience and a good distraction. Her dad smiles encouragingly at me.

Finally we get summoned to an examination cubicle, and I wave goodbye to my little audience girl.

"What happened to you, young lady?" asks the nurse, who is dressed in a floral top, baggy blue pants, and unusual plaid runners. Her stethoscope reminds me of watching Mom head off to work. I raise my head and try to look her in the eye as I spill my story, finishing with an embarrassed chuckle. "I guess I wasn't paying enough attention to the game!"

"We'll do a bit of checking and maybe an X-ray, but it looks like you have learned a lesson without too much damage. I need to stretch your eye open to check inside, but I don't think anything else will hurt."

"As long as there are no needles involved, I will be brave," I promise, and she returns my smile.

Waiting for a final OK from the doctor, we overhear a lot of stuff through the privacy curtains around us. We learn that the big, noisy family that arrived just after us is dealing with the death of a young man who fell from the thirteenth floor of the big apartment block just a block away.

I look at Mom and see raw grief reflected there. We are both right back in Fort McMurray, hearing the unmanageable words "I'm sorry, but your dad won't be coming home tonight. He was killed this afternoon."

It is a relief to leave the hospital, head aching, bruises growing by the minute, and embarrassed by my stupidity. But overshadowing everything is the newly opened wound of loss.

I vow to make a few changes. No more injuries for me.

I'm just a wreck. "Stick to what's simple," I say to myself. "The pool, the trampoline, and the hot tub. That's for me. No more trips to the ER. Maybe I will spend more time on schoolwork ... dream on!"

I'm enjoying the work in Ms Hetherington's class, health sciences. Mom calls it Nursing 101 and says I'm getting geared up for a nursing career.

Ms H is a former army nurse, and most of her stories are from the Wainwright Military Base. Perhaps that explains a lot about her teaching style of barking commands and employing explicit dramatics. She was quite intrigued with how awful I looked in class that first day after my ball-in-the-face episode, and she had some stories to top mine.

"I still can't believe it. Ms H will soon be Ms Somebody Else," whispered the class gossip, talking to her friend filing out behind me. "She's getting married!"

That's a little unbelievable at best, I think. She's not the marrying type, in my mind.

As Dad's quirky sayings popped into my head, a couple fit the scenario: "She's big enough to burn diesel and pack her own!" and "She's scary enough to make a freight train take a dirt road." She certainly scares the liver out of me at times. Dad had so many hilarious lines and was always coming up with new ones we'd never heard before. Laughter was his middle name, as Mom says, and it's one of the things I miss sooooooo much.

His comments were never said as taunts or to ridicule, they were just said with hilarity and a twinkle in his eyes.

"I miss your twinkle, Dad. I miss you."

Mom's always trying to remember a really funny poem he knew. She was always trying to learn it from him and would get him to recite it. But now it's too late. It began like this:

There was a boy; his name was Jim.
His friends were very good to him.
They brought him tea and cake and jam
And slices of delicious ham!

Then it went on about going out to the zoo and getting eaten by a lion slowly, bit by bit. It was a rather gory rendition, kind of like Ms H's classes. I'm surprised Mom likes it so much.

The whole crux of the matter, though, was that the lad disobeyed and "let go of nurse" when he was supposed to hold her hand. Maybe that is why Mom likes it; it's about obedience, and it mentions a nurse!

Our family is a celebration-fixation family. We celebrate everything. No one misses a funeral; they'll crawl over broken glass to honour someone that has died. But people are often too busy to attend a family reunion or wedding. Well, not us. We celebrate everything and try to involve everyone, even strangers. Mom always drags some poor soul in whether he or she wants to come or not, it seems to me. Whether it's Easter or Christmas or fresh bread day, it's time to share with others. She has sent me out to deliver fresh home-made potato doughnuts to neighbours we haven't even met.

We still celebrate the start of each school year by shopping for our favourite outfit, but it used to be Dad who always took us—a generous and seriously committed clothes-aholic. Apparently, when my parents got married, they each had a serious debt load; Dad's was at a menswear store, Cliff's Tog Shop, and Mom's was for her schooling. Yep, he had a soft spot for fashion, and that suited us just fine.

I see one of my last outfits we chose together hanging in the back of my wardrobe—a long-sleeved turtleneck crop top the colour of my eyes and high-waisted baggy jeans with a wide black belt.

Dad, I wish I could still wear this outfit anytime I need you near, I think. But I'm a few inches taller now, and my feet don't fit in those clunky-heeled shoes any more either.

I visualize the fun stores we were in at the Chinook Mall in Calgary. We took our sweet time and had a lot of laughs as I modelled myriad (I love that word) combinations.

"I miss you, Dad. Now and forever."

Alas, all I can think about right now is that Gina has decided she wants to go back to Caronport for grade ten and wants me to join her. My final year. My grad year. What do I think of that? What will Mom say? What will she do about both of us leaving and Torr, of course, being gone back to college for her second year? Mom will be totally alone except for Mr Man's occasional visits. *Will she be safe*? I wonder.

And what do I think of it?

I don't like change. I don't like moving. I don't like the unknown. I don't like decisions. I don't like arguing with Mom. I don't like losing the argument—and I will lose; that's a given. I haven't mastered the art of persuasion, and I loathe even thinking about it.

Well, what to do is a conundrum (one of Dad's favourite words). I'm feeling like a traitor. Yes, I'm a traitor to Mom if I choose to go away and a traitor to Gina if I chicken out and choose to stay home for my final year. I wish I had that "God told me this is what I need to do" direction some folks seem to have. I wish God would tell me what to do. Prayer is so nebulous. How do I know whether my sense of direction is from God or just my own desires?

Hmm. Maybe I'll think about this tomorrow. A little time in the hot tub with my book is in order. Good for the soul.

"N. C., are you coming to Caronport with me?" Gina breaks into my reverie with her very direct question. Where did she come from all of a sudden? I note she's getting so tall, and that short, saucy hairstyle looks so great on her. Her tiny nose piercing speaks of her nerve, too, I think. I wonder to myself what makes each of us so different.

Without waiting for my answer, she ploughs ahead excitedly. "I'm going to talk with Mom when she gets home from class. It's not her stats class today is it?" She sounds a little nervous. Our nerdy mom has signed up for a couple of spring sessions.

Gina doesn't get nervous very often, but we all know Mom gets a little stressed out with that stats class. She has almost quit it a couple of times. As always, she's doing well, but it has been a real challenge, and we all have to hear about it. We valiantly keep her going with our encouragement.

I silently hope it is stats class today. Maybe that will keep Gina from bringing up Caronport.

Oops, no such luck today. I've missed my chance of escape, and now Mom is coming in the back door. Borneo's streak of fur darts in ahead of her.

"Hi, Mom," Gina cheerily greets her while scooping the feline up lovingly.

"Hello, you guys. How was school?" Mom says.

"The usual," we both chorus. "How about you?" We exchange secretive looks.

"Yeah, how is stats class going?" Gina skilfully interrupts, directing the conversation.

"Oh, today was just a research data day with my partner, and it went very well," she informs us. "And I think we will complete by deadline. Wonder of wonders." She laughs and places her bookbag on a kitchen chair and turns to check the Crockpot housing our soon-to-be-enjoyed dinner.

I know Gina will seize this opportunity. Even I can see the wisdom in approaching the forbidden discussion at this very moment.

"That's great, Mom. You slugged it out to the bitter end, and I know you'll end up with a top mark as always. Hey, talking about school, I have a suggestion."

Without waiting for Mom to reply, and without taking a breath, she forges on. "I'm totally certain that I should go back to Caronport next fall and do my grade ten there. I do not want to go on to Lindsay Thurber or Hunting Hills either." Mom looks stunned and speechless, eyes wide and mouth agape. Gina, seeing her opportunity, wades in deeper. "N. C. wants to join me, and we can room together, and you'll have more free time to study your courses, and you can take care of transportation all in one trip to Saskatchewan, and—"

Mom finds her voice and her opinion, interrupting at last and looking stern with her eyes afire. "Holy cow, where does all this come from, Gina? When did you start thinking that way again? You are like Alberta weather, changing every five minutes. I thought you had this out of your system, and you know how I feel about it." She then fixes her fiery eyes on me. "Noelle-Cheri, what's this about you wanting to join her?"

It's my turn to be speechless.

Swallowing noisily, my eyes darting feverishly around the room for a persuasive thought, I plunge in, my voice a little squeaky as if caught in wrongdoing.

"Mom, Gina asked me a while ago, and I've been thinking about it. I've been thinking it might be a good idea, and Gina's only problem there earlier this year was that she got so lonely. With me there, that solves everything."

"Solves everything indeed!" Mom says sarcastically as she glares at us. She sounds disgusted. "I can't believe we're revisiting this, but if you two are serious, then so be it. Just give me a day or two to digest this, and we'll sit and talk it all out. Maybe this weekend is a good time." She heads out the door with "I need a walk."

"Great," we sheepishly chime together, relieved and surprised.

I'm a little numb as I think about what just transpired. Did I really say I wanted to go? *Do* I want to go? What have I done? I feel like I'd be leaving Dad even further behind, betraying him too. At least I have a couple of days to think it through again before Mom grills us on the plan or tries to dissuade us.

I feel Gina's eyes boring into me.

"Thanks a lot, Gina!" I seethe towards her when I am sure Mom is out of earshot. "What's the big idea directing the attention to me, as if it were all my idea?"

"Don't be a baby," she says as she attempts to minimize the role she dumped on me and follows me down the hall.

"A baby!" I retort, turning and posing to launch a chokehold on her. "Are you kidding me? I'm not being a baby. I'm just saying that wasn't fair. You can fight your own battle with Mom about Caronport. And I'm not going anyway." *There. That serves her right.*

"What do you mean you're not coming?" Gina asks furtively. "Just calm down. I thought it was all settled and you wanted to come. You said it would be fun to room together and be so independent and meet new kids. And new boys! You said you'd like to graduate from there and—"

"I also said I wasn't sure yet," I remind her snidely. "You know how Mom feels about the value of living at home in our school years and how I hate to argue and persuade. So don't dump it on me again." I point my finger in her face for further impact of my warning.

With that I escape to my room to finally change into my swimsuit and put an end to the discussion as if I had had the last word.

I know I have to make up my mind about Caronport soon though. I do want to go. I don't like the tension here when Mr Man visits—like the time he came home unannounced and I was chatting with Gina and her friends in the living room after school and listening to music. As usual, he went on to his bedroom without answering my hello or anything. In moments he came out again. "Turn that music down," he demanded as he stormed down the hallway, and towering over us, he glared down at us lounging on the living room rug before he retreated again to the bedroom. I felt scared and intimidated, but Gina stayed strong.

"Sure. OK," Gina complied politely and turned it down.

Very shortly, he bounded out of his room and out the front door. We all thought he was leaving again; he never tells us when he is leaving or returning or where he is going. I only know Mom is a different and more fun person when he is away.

Suddenly the front door opened, and in he came again, carrying his ghetto blaster under his arm. He keeps everything in his car boot—for quick getaway, I guess. With no comment or greeting, he retreated again to his room.

Immediately our ears were treated to a mega blasting of country-and-western music coming down the short hallway. We all just looked at each other, and no one said anything. We shut off our music and left the house. We left a note for Mom so she knew where to find us when she got home from work. We knew we wouldn't tell her why we all went to Sharon's home, though she might wonder, knowing I never hang with Gina's friends. Luckily, Mom never asked. When Mr Man appears, she doesn't function very well, and we can get away with a lot.

"I miss you, Dad."

I'm thinking maybe Caronport is a good idea for me too. I won't have to deal with Mr Man's moodiness and Mom's sadness. I won't have to tiptoe around all the landmines. I can pretend we still have a nice, normal family. And I know Gina and I would have a lot of fun. Mom is strong … I hope. *She'll be fine without us*, I rationalize. We'll be fine on our own, and I know she'll visit us lots. We'll come home as often as we can too.

There, it is all settled. I'll back Gina and make my own case too. I'm ready for the family meeting.

"Wish me luck, Dad!"

My decision means I'm going to complete grade twelve at private school in Caronport. Dorm living. Independence. New friends. New teachers. New rules. *Rules to bend, hopefully*, I think.

I glance around my cosy room and study the posters on the wall of the Backstreet Boys and Wayne Gretzky.

Memories are here of three years without you, Dad. If I go to Caronport, will I still hear you say, "We'll always be a family Mrs Mouse"? I shiver and begin to make note of the special things in my room that must go with me as I lock eyes with Dad in the picture I have of him on my dresser. "I love you, Dad," I mouth.

As Gina and I lounge in our eight-person hot tub, enjoying its warmth on a cool summer evening after a gentle rain, I get another information session from Gina.

What better way to spend our last night at home?

"Mrs Wutheridge is a stickler and a sneak," Gina cautions me. "Don't get caught doing anything out of the ordinary by her. She'll hang you by the thumbs and ask questions later," she details. "She doesn't like me, and she probably won't like you simply by association."

"She sounds formidable," I say, entering the fray. "Makes home sound like Eden. Maybe I should rethink this venture," I happily taunt.

"Don't be a chicken, N. C. You'll learn how to evade her and placate her. You're cleverer than me in that role. My problem is I always challenge her power-mongering. I'm a mouth for the underdog."

"Maybe she'll like us this year, Gina. We're older and wiser, and who can resist our charm? Maybe we can try out Fanny's ploy of batting our eyelashes and manufacturing tears." Gina rolls her eyes in disgust.

"No chancy, Mr Whalen," Gina admonishes with eyebrows arched and cheeks puffed out. I don't know who Mr Whalen is, and I'm sure Gina doesn't either, but it's a saying Dad had, and we both like it; it sounds so normal and definite. I know Dad went to a private Christian school, away from home, for high school, and I prop myself up with the thought.

"Mr Peabody, the vice principal, is a fun and fair fellow." Gina smiles her encouragement. "If any teachers send you off to him, just explain the situation, and he's very reasonable. Don't worry about those teachers. Some of them are dried up and sour and hate youth, but Mr Peabody evens things out."

"OK." *I can handle that*, I think as I listen carefully and try to picture Dad in his youth, going along this similar route. He obviously survived it well.

Gina continues her diatribe and warns, "Chapel is fine as long as you sit three quarters of the way back. If you sit at the back, they suspect you're up to no good and also that you slept in, which of course you did." She laughs infectiously, getting me laughing too. It feels so good to be laughing together and conspiring together; some of my loneliness fades. "But if you sit where I show you, it's usually a lot of fun with our friends, including great guys. Leonardo, this handsome dude from Spain, is lean, lanky, and totally hilarious. Gerard is a sports nut and also has a vehicle which he gallantly offers to drive us off campus, like to Moose Jaw or even Regina sometimes. Ben lives off campus, and his family hosts lots of youth parties."

My ears perk up at this point. *"Party" will be my middle name from now on*, I think as my mind wanders. I start to list my party outfits and remind myself of my ability to entertain with my quirky humour and craziness, which always get people laughing. Tosha's face flashes into my mind, and I recall all the crazy fun we used to have entertaining ourselves and our many friends with our wit. Life was manageable back then. Life was easy back then. Life was fun back then. *Why did you have to die, Dad? You ruined everything!*

"You'll need my pointers on how to work the least horrible student jobs, too."

Trying to refocus, I ponder my job experience. I did like teaching kids swimming, and I did like all my jobs at summer camp, I realize. Maybe there would be a job like that at Caronport.

Gina intercepts my thoughts and dashes my hopes. "There aren't any nice jobs at Caronport. And remember: never, never, never accept a place in the cafeteria milieu. Deadly!"

"Well, what about free time and weekend rules? Any bright spots in this gloomy picture?" I ask, pleading with my eyes.

"Actually, N. C., it is fun all the time—so many cool friends and laughter and pranks and just feeling all grown up. Plus you'll be my quad-mate."

"Your what?" I ask, scrunching up my face.

"My quad-mate! You and I each have a single bed in our room, but we are joined to another similar room with a bathroom in between. It makes for interesting mornings getting ready for school—actually, chapel first. We usually just put our coats over our PJs and skip breakfast. Then we run back and dress for class."

"Well quad-mate, you'd better be a worthy mate, 'cause I plan to take a stash of soup tins with me just in case you need a little adjusting now and then," I tease, reminding Gina of the time I threw one at her in youthful anger.

"Let's try to minimize civil war in the ranks and focus on the real enemy. Think we can do it?"

"Of course, little sister," I smoothly agree. I fold my hands in front of me and sit up straight, trying to emulate an angel, and say, "We will be an undaunted, immovable, remarkable, and gorgeous duo unlike anything that has ever, or will ever, entered the hallowed halls of Caronport High School and Caronport dorm."

I realize I'm glad to be heading off on a new adventure of dorm life and a private Christian High School.

I'm glad Mom was reasonable and listened to our request.

Overall, the family meeting went well. I usually hate them. Mom says the sum of the parts is greater than the whole. Whatever does that mean? I think she's trying to say we function best if we all join together as a group. Supposedly each of us has a valued opinion, and it contributes to the final decision. I've always thought my opinion rated pretty low and didn't make a difference in the least, but here I am off to Caronport, based on group ethics, not Mom's dictating. Maybe I am a believer in the process after all.

I quickly set to packing my treasured picture of Dad, my first priority, leaving it well protected between layers of my favourite clothing. *You're coming with me, Dad!*

I start singing the catchy refrain from the song Mom wrote for my sixteenth birthday:

My middlest, my middlest,
You're in the middle, you see.
My middlest, my middlest,
You are my lovely N. C.

BOOK 2

Victoria (Torr), July 1995

Monday

The countdown has begun in earnest now. Just six days till "D-Day". I guess if I were true to my French roots, I'd think *J-Jour*. Aren't I witty for having just woken—and no one near to catch my stab at humour either? I don't hear any sounds of life from the rest of the house yet. Well, the countdown for N. C. is well under way as well, but hers is not at the urgent stage yet, like mine.

As I lie buried in my pastel floral nest that matches the fabric-covered headboard and full-length draperies, my mind and heart are calm. Lying still, I marvel at the stabs of light criss-crossing the room; from any vantage point, it can sneak around the blinds. It is my own personal aroura borealis show. I try to imagine leaving all this familiarity behind.

Six days. That seems like a slow-as-molasses eternity at times, and at other times I wonder how we'll be ready in time! I'm so glad N. C. is home and walking the countdown with me. Gina will be home tomorrow; we'll have a houseful of women like old times. Yahoo! There's only our feline, Borneo, to present a token male presence.

That is soon to change, though, with both N. C. and me getting married—me this week and N. C. three weeks later.

I still can hardly believe it as I recall Serge's reluctance to be married and his change of heart. Last Christmas, after a bout of sickness and time for contemplation, he realized he wanted me in his life long-term.

Still, there was no formal engagement or marriage plan.

And to top things off, little sister N. C. said to me that same Christmas holiday while all of us were home, "Torr, Garrett and I are talking seriously about marriage."

"But ... But you just met him!" I stuttered, wide-eyed, and grabbed her arm, pulling her down beside me on the piano bench, right beside the brightly lit Christmas tree. "None of us know him. Or his family," I spluttered on, in bewilderment at the news.

"Torr, don't have a cow. I've known him four months already, and now you've all met him. Isn't he handsome? And tall and energetic and fun? And we won't be getting married for at least a year." She reached behind us, fingering a few happy, tinkling notes, eyes aglow and smiling back at me.

"Have you mentioned anything to Mom?" I asked with fear in my eyes, thinking Mom would indeed have a cow. We women of the family were on full alert. After experiencing the craziness of Mr Kreider in our lives these last few years, we were not very trusting! Mr Crazy had left our family, but we were still recovering from his temperamental volatility.

"Garrett is watching for a time to talk with Mom, but with how close to death her sister is, and those divorce papers served just last Thursday, it doesn't seem the time to load Mom up any more. And how cruel is it that those papers came on 28 December, the anniversary day of Dad's death?"

We sat in sober silence, and I tried to grapple with her news. I then heard her say quietly, "I know our happiness seems out of place at such a heavy time for Mom, but I wanted to let you know, sis." She reached for my hand.

Looking into her happy, dark eyes, I frowned and pressed my lips tightly together. Taking a deep breath, I covered our hands with my other hand as well, and I advised N. C. firmly, "You *have* to tell Mom about this. And the sooner the better!"

She did tell Mom later that very day, and we all cloistered together in Mom's bedroom and shared our worries about her hasty relationship. I'm rather certain our voiced concerns were not appreciated. Our need to protect her drove a wedge between us instead. She just wanted us to be happy for her.

Maybe none of us ever know what we are getting into; there are no guarantees that come with relationships, I suspect.

Mom had adjusted, and accepted the much shorter engagement even, and answered friends and relatives' flak for allowing her daughter to marry so young with "You marry when you find love! I can't dictate when that is for someone else. Hopefully she's made a good choice."

I glance at my clock to reassure myself I don't have to get up yet, turn over, and hug my special Grandma B. quilt. I've been teased that this raggedy, worn quilt will be part of my wedding bouquet!

I ponder my compulsion to have my wedding first. *I am two years older*, I think in justification.

But N. C. and Garrett had chosen their wedding date, and I was still waiting, waiting!

Then things all changed. I often think about that special romantic day.

I was looking after the home front for Mom, as she was out of country on her annual medical mission trip to Haiti. Serge was completing his fourth year of college to become a pastor and was doing his internship year in a church in Lethbridge.

I hadn't seen him for a few weeks but was hoping that maybe at Valentine's we'd see each other.

On 11 February, I came home from an outing with my friend, Randy, and there were well-wrapped flowers placed on the front step. I thought someone must have sent Mom flowers and not realized she was still away. But who would just leave them in this wintry weather? As I bent to rescue them and brush fresh fallen snow off the wrapping, I caught a movement out of the corner of my eye. There stood Serge in the flesh! I gaped at him standing in the shrubbery, looking a bit red-faced, a woolly toque accenting his smiling blue eyes, and his parka zipped to his cleft chin. He asked simply, "Am I welcome?"

I love replaying this scene in my mind.

"Of course, I stammered, as I struggled with the key in the lock. "Come on in out of the cold. You're covered in snow. How long have you been hidden behind there? Is Randy in on this prank? You guys are crazy!"

"It *is* a bit nippy out there," he commented, following me in. "I'm not sure the flowers have survived, but they were beautiful before I got stranded out there!"

"Shake the snow off your coat as best you can, Serge, while I put these in some water and hope they survive. They are truly lovely. Thank you so much!"

"Glad you like them, Torr. Take your time, but then join me in the music room; I have something else for you too," Serge mysteriously added.

Entering the music room, I saw Serge free a teddy bear from behind his back. I had been collecting Boyds Bears for years, but this one looked like soft corduroy in a deep burgundy colour. *Well, aren't I being spoiled and surprised all in one day?* I thought.

As I reached for it, I saw the glint of a gemstone dangling from its neck. My romantic fellow went down on one knee and asked beseechingly, "Victoria Jules Prescott, my beauty queen, I'm asking you to journey with me through life as my friend and wife. What do you think of that, sweetie?"

I'll never forget those words, and though my answer was already decided earlier, I stood speechless in the face of this spectacular scenario, just staring at him and then blinking rapidly with my mouth a bit slack. Still I had no voice.

I realized he had looked a little stressed and uncomfortable when he arrived, and now I understood why!

"Yes, I'd like that, Serge," I finally stated simply.

This meant he must have already managed the "get parental permission" step. We all knew Dad would have required any serious suitor to have the father–son talk if marriage was on the table. Mom had decided to accept the surrogate role.

Serge admitted he had squeezed in a clandestine meeting with Mom before she left for Haiti.

"You sly fox! How did you manage that? And how did it go?" I stumbled over my surprise and questions as we sat on the piano bench together, admiring the glittering ring on my finger. Before he could answer, we counted the number of colours emanating from it as the sunshine struck it; there were blues, greens, and reds.

"She gave me permission to ask for your hand, so I think it must have gone OK," he reasoned, giving me a self-satisfied look with raised brows, pursed lips, and chin tilted up while puffing out his chest and hooking his thumbs on his upper shirt as if stretching braces. "Mainly, your mom stressed the *imperative* of loving you, her daughter, more than hockey and sports, participatory or on TV!" Serge mimicked Mom's stern voice of conviction and then mimed shooting and scoring an imaginary goal into the brick fireplace.

Laughing, I replied, "I'm surprised you agreed to that, my consummate sports fiend! Lucky for you, you've already passed the prerequisite of playing guitar."

We girls all know that any man entering the family must be able to play guitar; we've all been indoctrinated on that count. Mom loves music, and guitars are portable and therefore more flexible socially; they can accompany any event, indoors or out.

Our little whirlwind romantic interlude was over too quickly, as I needed to head to work and he had the long, snowy drive back to Lethbridge ahead of him.

It was short and sweet and oh so memorable, like the saying "It's not the number of breaths you take but what takes your breath away."

With that sparkler on my left ring finger, a breathless song in my heart, and lightness in my step, I headed to work without the usual drudgery. No foul customer could rain on my parade that day—or should I say "snow on my parade"? I felt loved and special.

Taking another glance at my bedside clock, I jump out of bed, realizing I've dawdled too long in my reverie. I will have to forego my morning run. I have my final dress fitting, and I need to meet with our photographer once more in just over an hour. I need to get ready and catch a bite of breakfast too. I am ravenous!

I wish Serge could be here to help finalize things. He's so easy-going; I know he'll approve what I choose, but I hate making important decisions by myself.

Our three years of dating gives me confidence he's the special guy for me, despite our differences. My taste for classical music and Serge's love of country has been a fun mix as we've chosen wedding music. I've learned an appreciation for his music, and I think he has grown in tolerance for mine. Love is our catalyst for new learning.

Happiness wells up inside me as I think of Serge, and I visualize him standing serious and handsome in a tuxedo, in awe and love, as his twinkling blue eyes draw me to the front of the church, floating dreamily down the aisle while the violin plays our romantic piece, augmenting the solemnity and beauty of the occasion, which is now just five days away! I'm reminded my sisters call me the family romantic.

Our Fort Mack friend, Loyal, will be back from his Singapore holiday after all, which means we can indeed add violin to our wedding service; this will be special for my grand entrance. I get gooseflesh thinking about that music, and I count my lucky stars he is free to be here. He has sent the sheet music for our pianist, and it looks really complex; I'm glad I don't have to accompany him! I hope my cousin, who has promised to be our pianist, can handle the changes Serge and I have decided on.

Driving to the bridal shop for my fitting, I turn briefly to Mom with a questioning frown at the first red light and say, "I think something is bothering N. C." I look back at the light and shake my head. "I can't believe she backed out on joining us for this fitting. She seems distracted, or angry even. And she's definitely avoiding any talk about Dad."

"I'm not sure what's going on in her head right now, Victoria, but I agree she seems distracted. She has never been comfortable talking about her dad, or more accurately her loss of him," Mom says thoughtfully, looking out the window, likely not even seeing the passing houses. And after a pause, she says more quietly, "I have not been able to fill her father's role of confidante, and I feel bad about that. They just had a natural understanding, and she lost that, big time."

"Maybe Garrett will be able to fill that role for her now," I say as I turn into a parking spot, disappointed that our conversation is interrupted.

I come out of the change room modelling my gown on the mirrored platform, and I see myself from all angles, with infinite reflections of shimmering and light. I look towards Mom and read her eyes of love and pride.

"You are a vision of loveliness, Victoria," she says solemnly.

Anna, the dressmaker, fusses and fiddles and declares she needs to take in the waist a tiny bit more. She shows us again how to button the train into a bustle and asks me to return for pickup tomorrow morning.

Tuesday

Again I wake early, and snuggling in my special quilt, I enjoy a time of daydreaming and thinking about how N. C. and I will be heading in different directions. She and Garrett are planning on buying a restaurant in his hometown in Saskatchewan. They plan to settle there and make their mark in the world—pretty adventuresome for sure. Unbidden, I'm reminded of those half-cooked meatballs N. C. served us a few years back. Maybe I should give Garrett a little warning that his bride-to-be is not too interested in cooking!

Humour bubbles in my soul at this thought, and I realize I'm not going to get back to sleep. I get out of bed and slip my feet into well-worn mules. Wrapped in my long Malibu-blue terry robe, I twist my long, thick, curly mane into a top-knot and pad my way up to the music room. I cross over to our shiny black baby grand, displayed elegantly in the bay window, and open up the sheet music Loyal has sent me. The stately, mature trees outside, screening the house, provide privacy for me.

I have faithfully taken lessons and practised piano a good dozen years, and I now valiantly try to tease out the haunting tune of Loyal's sheet music before me. Mom and N. C. can awaken to a simplified version as I struggle on. I've always loved my childhood memories of listening to Mom play gentle tunes on the piano or guitar when we girls had to head to bed. Now I can return the favour in reverse. I chuckle as I wonder if it will be as well received at this morning hour.

"N. C., wake up, sleepyhead." I bend low and whisper in her ear and try to pull her pillow out from under her for good measure.

"Go away, you pest!" she hisses, grabbing her pillow back.

"I need you to get ready, N. C." I persist. "Did you forget I'm going to my final fitting and get to bring my dress home? I really want you to come. I'll treat you to a late breakfast after," I promise with sugar in my voice. "Your restaurant of choice."

"I need a bigger bribe than a breakfast, dear sister," she mumbles from under her pillow. "And I'm not in the mood for your dress fitting"

"Whoa there. What's up with you this morning; want to talk about it?"

"No. Just need my space; that's all." She burrows deeper under her covers.

"All right, then. I can give you space," I say testily. "See you later."

Determined to not let her mood pull me down, I head out to complete my tasks for the day and check each off as I accomplish them. I can't wait to try on my beautiful gown again and bring it home. Hopefully N. C. will be in a better mood then or will be ready to talk about what's eating her.

Returning a couple of hours later, excited and energetic, I grab the ringing phone, breathless. "Hello?"

"Hello to you too, Hooper Chuck," Serge says, teasing me with one of my dad's crazy pet names.

"I'm so glad I didn't miss your call. I just got in the back door! Good timing, eh?"

"Always good timing. That's me. How are things going?"

"Very well. Just brought my dress home even. It's beautiful!"

"No, you are beautiful."

"Well then, I will be doubly beautiful." I laugh. "Is everything with your family going well?" Knowing his mom is often unwell and finds travel very difficult, I worry she might not come.

"No problems yet. I can still get there by Thursday, late afternoon, and the rest of my family Friday, in time for the rehearsal dinner. Taking two days will break it up for my mom."

"How is work at the mine going? Is tomorrow your last shift?"

"The money has been good, but I'm so glad to be done at the mine."

"Torr!" N. C. yells as I hear her bounding in the front door.

"Oh, I'd better go, Serge. N. C. just got home."

"Yes, I hear her," he laughs with good humour, understanding our sister connection over the last few years. "I'll call again tonight. I love you."

"Love you too. Bye."

As I turn, N. C. stands with hands on hips, glaring at me.

"What's up, N. C.?" I ask, suddenly concerned.

"I walked to the bridal shop; need I say anything more!" Her eyes are laughing, belying her voice tone. "The exercise did me good. Sorry I missed your fitting," she adds apologetically.

Glad to hear her in a better mood, I don't press her for more explanation.

Smiling forgiveness and changing the subject, I say brightly, "Gina should be home by this evening."

"We ladies will all be together for these few days," she agrees soberly.

"We ladies, all missing Dad," I add.

Turning abruptly, she calls over her shoulder brightly, "I have things to do and places to go and people to see!"

Wednesday

With both N. C. and me getting married within three weeks of each other, our home has been a high-energy place for some time now; much change is a-happening to this all-girl family.

To mark the change, we girls have a special thank-you day planned for Mom, so there is no early-morning piano practice etude or lyrical sonata to wake the household today. We want to treat her to a surprise drive out to Ellis's Bird Farm and Tea House.

"Torr, do you think we'll get lost this time?" N. C. asks.

"Not a chance, N. C." My confident blue eyes meet her questioning hazel ones. "Now that we know to watch for that skyscraper grain elevator, how could we miss our way?" I declare, full of bravado. We learned on our last visit that it is the oldest standing seed elevator remaining in Alberta. "And our destination is well signed from that place onward."

"That long, welcome lane sporting the world's largest collection of bluebird houses will be the next clue," N. C. reminds me.

"Agreed. I think we'll be OK, and I'm excited to go back there again. It's been a while, and it has such good memories for us tea-time, country-exploring ladies!" I say jauntily.

We always explore the wildlife gardens and paths and treasures. But what brings us back again and again is the heritage farmhouse converted into a tea house serving both savoury and sweet delectable treats.

Good fortune is with us today, and we snag the secluded round corner table with windows burrowed right into the lush, thick shrubbery featuring bird activity on two sides of us—a perfect spot for us to chatter away ourselves.

"What a crazy surprise this is," Mom splutters after we order savoury scones and tea, saving dessert choices for a bit later. "We should probably be busy getting wedding things done, though."

"Everything is going smoothly, Mom. Relax. We just want to say thank-you, and we want to have a teeny time to celebrate the four of us single ladies before *someone* gets married off!" N. C. teases.

I'm sure she's trying to get a rise out of me because of my obsession to be the first married, simply because I'm oldest. Hey, I am two years her senior, so I feel justified. Even though my wedding is just three weeks sooner than hers, it makes a difference in my mind.

Changing the focus, I say, "I woke this morning with memories of Dad's crazy childhood stories he used to tell so vividly. You guys remember, right?" I lean forward, gazing at everyone hopefully.

"Well," Gina starts, pausing for a moment with pursed lips for dramatic effect, "one I really like is the one about him riding home after Sunday church in the country, with kids crammed in the backseat. Seatbelts were not even invented yet! Going around a corner, someone bumped the doorknob, and the door sprang wide. Those vehicles had a reverse action to what we're used to these days and were rightly called suicide doors. Our eight-year-old dad went flying out, tumbled over and over in the weedy ditch, and without even stopping, commenced a tear after the disappearing vehicle, afraid he was lost forever!"

"Like an energized Forrest Gump, I'm picturing," I say, also remembering Dad's story.

"Dad liked to tell me the one of disobeying the directive to go to bed when he had asked to accompany his dad to the field one more time," N. C. chimes in while attempting to mimic an impish face of a young boy.

Amidst our laughter, she continues. "He sneaked out into the grain truck and hid quietly. When his dad came out from supper to head back to the field, he threw his pitchfork randomly into the back of the truck. As luck would have it, Dad got a pitchfork tine in the butt! The plan of being a stowaway came to an unexpected and premature exposure when he let out a resounding *yelp!* He was unceremoniously sent to the house for his mom to bind his wounds."

As our laughter quiets down, I finally add my memory. "An unbelievable favourite of mine is his tractor incident with his oldest brother who was returning from the field and driving up the driveway. Dad ran alongside and jumped up to ride upon the large wheel housing. A certain unseen and unexpected bump in the road bounced him forward and off balance, back down on the road in the path of the big tractor. His brother could not avoid running over him, right over his hips. Dad was unable to move his legs, so family help was secured to haul him into the house. There he lay for a few days, till feeling and mobility gradually returned. No ambulance. No doctor. No X-rays, CT scans, or intervention. It sounds so archaic, like the Stone Age or something. That's what makes it one of my favourite stories, I think."

Amidst our renewed laughter, I wonder to myself what his existence is like now too. He didn't know his time with us would be so short. He didn't know others would have to come together and try to fill the gaping hole he'd leave. Would he have been stricter, less fun? Would he have crammed in more career experience? Would he have bought us even more gifts? Would he not have made us eat those half-raw meatballs? He was so determined not to cook or make meals that he championed us making them and even enforced the eating of that unfortunate, sorry meal N. C. made!

At the risk of spoiling our celebratory mood, I blurt out, "I'm often trying to imagine what my life would look like now if Dad hadn't died. Do any of you find yourselves doing that too?" The prolonged silence that follows speaks volumes.

I calm myself, remembering Mom telling us that you know you've asked a good question when people don't respond quickly but pause to think. As I clasp my hands on my lap, my eyes gently roam around the circle of my family and back again in the silence and anticipation as I wet my lips and slow my breathing.

Gina, brave soul, is again first to wade in, though she does so tentatively.

"I know I actually do that often, but nothing concrete comes to me. It scares me that I have trouble even remembering what it was like when Dad was still in my life." Silent tears appear, but she continues. "Maybe it's like what you said, Mom; blocking our memory of something bad also blocks our good memories. Will I ever get more memory back?"

N. C. is folding and refolding her napkin meticulously and tapping her foot like a metronome. I feel threatening sparks coming from her discomfort in this turn of the conversation, and I suspect my verbose sister is approaching this conversation with uncharacteristic muteness.

My throat constricts, and I feel the familiar tightness in my chest as I feel my own sadness, but also that of my mom and sisters.

Our eyes all swivel towards Mom, as if she can direct us somehow.

"Girls," she starts, but she doesn't continue. "Hmm," she tries again. "That's a sobering question, Victoria." Silence again.

Then she starts a third time, and I hold my breath and glance at my sisters. Gina meets my look, but N. C. has her eyes on her plate. "We all enjoy the fast-track Scrabble game, right?" We nod collectively, even N. C., and Mom continues. "We turn all those letter tiles face down, mix them all up, and pick up five. Once someone can create real words with their meagre tiles and calls out, 'Pick one,' we each quickly grab another tile and, bit by bit, keep on making real words from the gibberish of letters."

I'm listening intently and frowning in concentration as I continue to nod lightly, hopefully encouraging her.

"It seems to me," she says hesitantly, "there is nothing about our life now that we can recognize from our life with your dad. The scrabble letters have all been rethrown. We each have had, and continue to have, the task of trying to create real words from the gibberish of random letters we find ourselves among. Maybe each of us has picked our five letters and has been creating, and I know we are all making an effort to help each other recreate meaning too." After another pause and a sip of her tea, she again speaks uninterrupted. "In our past life, words like 'friends', 'Mom' and 'Dad', 'education', 'career', 'continuity', 'family', and 'home' all had comfortable meaning and knowing. After another pause; a deep, audible inhalation of breath; and a couple of teeth biting her lower lip, she forges on. "In our new life, the words seem to be spelled differently or have different meanings. Or they might not even exist any more." She furrows her brow. Then, looking directly at N. C. and me, she says, "Victoria, Noelle-Cheri, you have Serge and Garrett in your lives now, and you've chosen a path of marriage and a future family of your own."

"We certainly have," I concur, turning to look N. C. full on, and I smile conspiratorially and give her a quick little shoulder hug. She seems to resist my sisterly gesture.

"A big change I see," Mom continues, "is that postsecondary education and career pursuits are on the back burner. Actually, I see that for all of us, relational efforts are our focus." Turning to look directly at Gina, she gently continues. "Gina, since your dad died, you have come from childhood as a grade sixer and are now a graduate, soon to be eighteen—adulthood. But please know you have inner strength from love and time from your dad, even though you can't remember much; it's in your heart and neuronal pathways and DNA!" She affirms this with conviction and raised eyebrows.

We remain silently drinking in Mom's words.

She changes her position slightly, crossing her legs and rearranging her napkin on her lap; then she continues in our silence of wanting to hear more.

"We're all still floundering on our new path," she asserts, "but we've all made some progress. We are fortunate to have wonderful family support and a good number of committed friends. And for me, it's a comfort to know God understands my sorrow. In fact, I think that is one way in which we are created in God's image; we have the capacity to love much, and with that comes the pain of loss associated with loving deeply."

Our busy server bustles over and apologizes for taking so long. The timing is perfect, and we relish the distraction and opportunity to change tack.

I order, breaking our reflective mood. "I'll have the Saskatoon pie with whipped cream, please. And Earl Grey tea."

After we all make our special requests and have eaten our delicacies, Mom declares, "A walk through the wilderness paths is in order, I think."

The beauty and freshness of the outdoors renews my spirit, and I head home thoughtful but more light-hearted.

It was a special time together this afternoon, and I feel wiser and more mature being armed with family time shared. Now I have just two more sleeps till my special day—my wedding day with Serge!

Thursday

I race to answer the front doorbell and am rewarded with my gallant fiancé unexpectedly being an hour early.

"I knew it was you," I greet Serge smugly, and I throw my arms around his neck.

"It's good it was me, considering the warm welcome." He laughs.

"How did you make that long trek so quickly?"

"Pedal to the metal, my dear. Actually, I got to McBride last night, stayed with family friends, and left early this morning. Only stopped for gas. Wanted to surprise you."

"Well, you did surprise me. I love it. Do you need a sandwich or something?"

"I had a packed lunch, just like a workday, but what I do need is to stretch my legs. Can we go for a walk first thing?"

"Perfect. I'll just leave a note for whoever is looking for me, and we can vamoose."

Heading out the back door, we see N. C. in the hot tub, reading a book.

"Serge is here already, and we're going for a walk," I call out to her over the noise of the jets. "Not sure when we'll be back."

She gives a thumbs up and a wave in acknowledgement, quickly returning her attention to her book.

Opening the back gate, I say, "I want to go this way and show you where I do my morning runs. We can follow the ridge path, and it leads to the network of trails through the treed areas all through the city."

Walking hand in hand, we chatter nonstop; we have so much catching up to do.

"Serge, look; there's a playground. I've never noticed it when out running. Let's sit on the swings and talk a bit."

Two swings accommodate us in a world of our own as we gently move back and forth in sync.

"Serge, this swinging experience is like a Dad connection. When we lived on our acreage, he made a big rusty-pipe-looking contraption that withstood all our antics. Two swings of old tyres were suspended, one horizontal and the other vertical, using just a quarter of a tyre—one you couldn't fall out of. Gina must have still been a baby when he made it. That horizontal one, Dad would wind it round and round and let it go for the craziest ride a kid could want. Of course, the supporting side bars were our monkey bars!" I'm breathless when I finish speaking, wrapped up in my memories.

"I can hear joy in your voice, Torr."

"Oh, and the tree house he built for us," I say as I plant my feet firmly, stopping my swing's momentum. "How could I forget! It was down a narrow path through the trees, just before the chicken yard,"

I charge on, barely taking a breath and visualizing the scary vertical climb up the tree trunk to the platform up in the big branches.

"Thanks for being a good listener, Serge," I say as I wrap my arms around him, feeling safe. "How I wish I could tell Dad thank you. I bet I never did." I end in lament.

"Let's continue our walk, pretty lady," Serge says as he takes my hand.

Walking in silence, I lead him to the creek trails where we skid down the grassy bank and sit listening to the gurgling creek.

"Torr, is everything set for the resort at Fairmont for our honeymoon week?"

"Yes, I have the confirmation and contact information packed already. How about arrangements for our adventure in the Queen Charlotte Islands after?"

"George and Jen have said we definitely can borrow their tent trailer, and I have a hitch on the car now, so all is a go." He looks questioningly at me.

"I can't believe I'm going mushroom picking on a strange island—and with a new husband to boot," I say, hoping I sound confident. "And who would even make such a suggestion?" I ask, giving him a playful shove.

"Do I detect a quiver of fear, my dear?" he asks, and he pauses, holding both my hands gently. We should make good money and pay down some student loan debt and have a fun adventure together."

"I can't even picture it, Serge. Can you?"

"No, not really," he says, leaning back on both elbows and gazing towards the creek. "We're just jumping—free fall, I guess, but jumping together. What do you say?" He turns to face me intently.

"I say we must be crazy, but at least we'll be together. I like that." We embrace, falling over in the grass together.

Walking back home, Serge says, "N. C. seems different today. Is everything OK with her and Garrett?"

"I think so, but I'm concerned too. She hasn't opened up about anything yet. Wedding jitters, maybe? Hey, what about your family? Is your mom doing OK? Is the trouble with the tuxedos figured out?"

"Ah, one question at a time, my girl," he pleads, and he holds both hands up in surrender. "I will head over to the tux shop right after this. Hopefully Mom and Dad are getting a good start on the drive today. They will call me at my hotel tonight with an update."

Friday

Unable to sleep in this morning like I planned, I realize I hear someone else playing the piano. *Doesn't sound like Mom. It won't be Gina. Must be N. C.*

Donning my comfy robe and slippers, I head to the music room and gently squeeze myself onto the bench beside her.

Turning to me with a flash in her eyes, she says "What?"

"Nothing. Just enjoying the morning wake-up you're providing, N. C. How are you this morning?"

After a long pause while she plays quite a few bars and I wonder if I should leave, she says heatedly, "I just don't want everyone mournful and morose during this time. We are getting married, Torr!" she exclaims, giving me a severe look with her chin tucked and eyes aflame. "It's a happy time. Remember? It's a new beginning. It's a celebration. I want mine to be a normal wedding; that's all." As she concludes, she strikes a strong final major cadence, which resounds throughout the house, for emphasis.

"Meaning no talks about Dad? No tears?" I qualify suspiciously.

"Precisely," she declares, nodding emphatically and favouring me with another full-face challenging glare.

"N. C., what are you afraid of?"

"I'm not afraid of anything. I'm just telling you I want a normal, happy, celebrative wedding day"—she plays another strong major chord—"not a mournful occasion." She makes her point with a loud minor cadence.

"I hear you loud and clear, N. C. I just don't think I can turn off that big part of me and pretend I'm not missing Dad on this very momentous occasion. I can't promise no tears, N. C.; they are friends of mine," I tease to lighten the discussion.

"They aren't friends of mine, Torr; they bring me down."

"I will do my best, little sister. You have my word," I promise with a shoulder hug as I depart. "Keep playing, N. C. It's beautiful."

I arrive early at my aunt's house to help set up for the rehearsal luncheon. We want simple fare and an informal time for two families to connect. The well-treed yard guarantees privacy and spaces for small groups to nestle, while the large curved patio and flowerpots lend a welcoming atmosphere. As we set up a serving table with a lovely draping cloth, I eye the sky.

"Auntie, do you think we're in for a drenching this evening?"

"Possibly. We'd better keep the rest of everything under the covered sections for now, just in case," she advises with a worried frown. "We'll leave all the candle accents and dishes in their boxes; don't want them to all blow away if a squall arises. We have no control over the weather, but I know we will have a good time," she promises enthusiastically.

Within two hours, a rogue storm has darkened the sky, stripped trees, and broken limbs off. The city park's beauty has turned to grotesque mayhem, and underpasses are flooded. My plans are in shambles too.

Arriving at the church for rehearsal, we find the power is out in this part of town. Our busyness grinds to a halt, and our skyrocketing tension starts an even steeper climb.

Then jokes and laughter take over as I hear a groomsman tease, "Hey, Serge, is this your ploy to chicken out and stay a bachelor?" This comes from Clint, who has vowed to never marry.

"It would take more than a little hail and thunder, power outage, or flood to scare me off," Serge rebuffs gallantly before he sticks out his chest and reaches for my hand.

"At least none of us drowned in the underpass," says Grandma, who cites a similar storm in Saskatchewan that claimed the life of a woman trapped in her car.

Stunned by this news, I quickly change the subject. "The city park has been decimated by the hail. We won't be able to have pictures there tomorrow." My voice catches, and I can't go on.

"But the studio will do just fine as the alternative," Serge reminds me, and he squeezes my hand.

A few candles are found, and Serge's dad, our officiating minister, gives a few encouraging words and instructions. Everyone listens intently, and one run-through for tomorrow's service seems sufficient.

Relieved to get way from the eerie darkness inside the sanctuary, we blink in the bright sunlight and breathe deep the fresh smell of the recent storm. Big trees on the church property are all still intact, and I give thanks for that as we walk on their carpet of stripped leaves.

Knowing Auntie's yard is decimated and unsafe to use, everyone voices a suggestion for a changed venue for our rehearsal dinner.

"We could go for a wiener roast at Kin Canyon and use a bunch of broken branches for our fire," suggests Randy.

"Or a motorcade drive-through at Dairy Queen," laughs Serge

I see my aunt drive up, and we all listen intently, hoping she has a solution.

"I just talked with the Mandarin Dynasty restaurant, and they are happy to have us all over there instead of the home delivery we had planned," she announces with bright eyes and hands open in joy. "How's that sound?"

Hungry shouts of agreement answer her, and we all pile into our vehicles and follow the lead car, who hopefully knows the way.

I lay my head on Serge's shoulder and heave a big sigh, wondering what's going to happen next. Serge squeezes my shoulder, and I begin listening to all the fun banter of our friends riding with us. I begin to relax and determine to shed the disappointment that was taking root.

Saturday

There is a roaring in my ears that is shutting out all other sound. It is getting nearly impossible to ignore the pain in my side, and I know I am slowing my pace from oxygen-starved muscles. *This can't happen. I'm so close; can't lose him again. Keep running. I can do it. Did I call out? Please hear me. Which way did you go?*

I am sure it was him I saw—just a glimpse, a profile.

Gasping and dragging air into my lungs during a brief halt, I frantically flash my eyes left then right. This choice is critical, I know. If I choose the wrong way, I'll lose him. "Go with your first gut feeling," I hear—a directive from my past.

I choose left but find nothing. I plead futilely with people on the street, realizing I don't even know their language.

"Have you seen a tall man with dark hair and a moustache, blue eyes, and wearing a dark sport jacket?" Surely someone knows enough English to help me.

No one helps. They talk about other things; I think it is Spanish they're speaking. A small music group and dancers with lurid masks appear, circling me and taunting me. They spin me around and around from person to person as though I'm part of their dance routine. I'm overpowered and helpless to regain control. I feel faint, and I hear someone weeping.

There are tears soaking my pillow as I wake from my recurring nightmare of the last six years, though it's been a long time since I last had it.

I lie still, grateful I haven't wakened anyone, and let my heart rate return to normal. God, thank you for these tears; I've learned the value of the regular release of pain through tears. Mom says none of them are wasted or insignificant; according to the scriptures, God collects them all in a bottle. What a beautiful picture of caring. But I hope my eyes don't get all red and puffy from this indulgence!

I feel exhausted, but I slowly become aware of person, place, and time. I smile reluctantly at the phrase that pops into my mind.

"Person, place, and time." It is a mantra I've heard Mom speak of when assessing people's states of consciousness, but I find it serves to calm me when I'm upset. "What is your name, Torr? Where are you? What time is it—or day or month or year?" If I can answer those basic questions, surely I can begin my day.

I take the time to lie still and let my mind drift to those unresolved areas that surface unbidden at the strangest and most unwelcome times, thankful I haven't disturbed my roommates.

I don't know what triggers them. Obviously this, my wedding day, must be one of the triggers! Or perhaps the trigger was the destructive storm last night.

I know N. C. refers to what happened to us, six years ago, as a tornado. The other day, I decided to research the word. I was stunned to find out that a tornado is accompanied by loud noise—a sound like that of a freight train! So I guess her choice of a descriptive word for our experience is very fitting. *Good one, N. C.*, I think; *you are a natural writer!* I must tell her what I've discovered.

The blanket of night is still around me, so I will lie here and enjoy the stillness of pre-dawn and the gentle sounds of a house at rest. I know I won't get back to sleep after having that dream.

Disjointed thoughts flash through my mind—pieces of memories. I always replay the arguments I had with Dad and feel guilt afresh. Why can't I focus on something else? Why do those few times of arguing take the forefront? I guess we didn't get to finish our debates. *I hope you forgive me, Dad. I forgive you.* I wonder if we would still be debating. Now, six years later, would I hold my own opinions more maturely, be less antagonistic, accept our different perspective more graciously?

My thoughts wander to Mom too. I think that, being the eldest, I have been allowed into her confidence and shared in her grief journey somewhat, and I've even had some glimpses into the stress around Mr Kreider in her life.

I have no wisdom for her. I just listen. I know that is what helps me—someone who will listen to me and hear my sadness, not try to explain it away or press me to minimize or deny my pain and fragility. Serge is a good listener and never seems uncomfortable with my stories and frequent need to talk about my dad. I think Serge's gentle spirit and sense of humour, so like those of my dad, are part of his attractiveness.

I'm reminded of the patience and humour Dad showed while teaching me to drive. Mom had relinquished that responsibility totally after a frightful episode in the Sawridge hotel parking lot. I can still hear Mom yelling, "*The brake, the brake, the brake!*" as I roared backwards across the parking lot. I did get stopped before reaching any parked vehicles, but not before Mom decided to have Dad take on my driver ed responsibility.

Serge has listened attentively to me talk about that fateful day the RCMP came to our house in Fort Mack when I was home alone, doing last-minute Christmas break homework. Everyone else had gone uptown, shopping for the upcoming New Year's Day groceries. I was terrified. He was a tall, daunting figure in his official attire, all dark and bulky, guns and all. He looked so severe and serious but wouldn't tell me what he wanted,

"I will wait in my car till your mom gets back home," he stated curtly. That was a long and tortuous wait. I felt as if I were in one of N. C.'s horror movies. My mind seemed incapable of guessing what an RCMP would want with my mom. There couldn't be a good reason. But I couldn't let my mind specify an actual guess; I just felt a cold, nameless dread. I tried to will my mom to come home soon, yet at the same time I was hoping she wouldn't, because it would confirm the potential terror to come.

Nothing could have prepared me for the devastating news dropped on us that day like a bomb. And I was one of the surviving wounded. Maybe some of my woundedness is well scabbed over now, but it seems it doesn't take much to reopen it, causing me to leak fresh tears.

Mom has been active in her new role of facilitating grief recovery groups, and I think that when I get settled in my new life as a married woman, I will take her recent advice and find a group.

She counsels that it doesn't matter how many years have passed; what's important is recognizing the need and seeking support.

My room is fully bright now with the day's light, and I hear muted sounds from the kitchen area. It's probably Mom starting preparations for my celebrative breakfast. This is a very important day.

With a glance around my room, I realize my friend and bridesmaid Randy has sneaked out to the shower without me noticing. Yes, I think I hear her singing in the shower. That means I'm next in line. I hear the soft breathing of Randy's cherubic little baby, Chloe, snuggled asleep in the playpen near my bed; she's too small and needy to stay home with Daddy yet. Dawn-Ray, my other friend and bridesmaid, is still snoozing on her floor mat—luck of the draw last night. My sisters make up the rest of the wedding attendants, so they have their own comfy beds for the night and are certain to still be sleeping!

It is so good to have Gina home for this special week of last-minute details and fun flurry! She is my baby sister and is only seventeen, but she is definitely no slouch when it comes to getting things done. She is a competent driver somehow too, so I have tasked her with lots of errands. Mom lucked out there. N. C. won't even get her learner's licence, and I have had a few fender-benders, but Gina takes to it like a duck to water. I am reminded how different we sisters are on many levels. Gina is the *get things done* gal. N. C. is the saucy *have fun* gal. And I'm … Oh yeah. I'm dubbed the *romantic* gal.

Today I embark on the mysterious title of *Mrs*—married woman. The ferocity and surprise of last night's storm still chills me, and I hope it isn't a portent of my married life to come. Butterflies in my stomach start their launch and cannot be denied or distracted. Getting rid of them is not feasible. Randy is an *experienced* married lady already, so maybe she can keep me focused and confident.

She and I have similar fair complexions, but Randy has enough red highlights in her wavy hair to be a strawberry blond. She's a little taller than my five feet four inches and has kept her schoolgirl figure even with the recent delivery of her daughter. I love her sparkling blue eyes and sunshiny disposition. And I especially like her daredevil attitude.

She, Dawn-Rae, and I have been such close buds over these last few years of work and college. So many goofy pranks flood my mind: sneaking off campus (and getting caught a couple of times); doughnut runs (Robin's Donuts) into Swift Current, a forty-minute drive; and even legitimate activities like football and college choir and riding horses all over the Pambrun, Saskatchewan, countryside. We once rode most of the way to the US border. Dawn-Rae, lucky lady, is from a horse ranch in southern Alberta, but I've had experience wrangling for a summer camp near Neilburg, Saskatchewan, for many years. I love horses and love teaching kids to ride. Mom finds it terrifying to think of me in charge of all those kids and managing some very spirited mounts. It's always nice to realize you can impress your own mother with your grown-up skills.

But the best times we had as friends were our all-night talks, thanks to communal dorm life; there's so much to discuss and figure out. For instance, there is the time Randy plopped herself down beside me as I sat cross-legged on my bed, trying to format an essay outline on gender roles in the modern church. It was coming due in two days, and I was still wrestling with a format.

"Why the frown, Torr? A sour note from your beau? Pun intended," she jibed.

"I'm stuck on this crazy assignment, you silly girl, about our roles in the church these days. Church history classes and classes in the history of music in the church are fascinating courses, and I find the assignments manageable, even enjoyable. But this ... this one has me bogged right down. Have you written yours?"

"Nah, haven't started. Lots of time yet," Stated my off-the-cuff roomie, while chewing noisily on a big red apple.

I envy her casual approach to assignments; I'm too serious, I guess.

"Just write what you believe, Torr, even it if differs from the hard line here at the school or, especially, our friend Carol. She likes to dictate our thoughts and behaviours." She pauses to wipe her chin of the apple's juices. "But really, we are each accountable; we live our lives based on what we understand, not what she has decreed. She's a harsh taskmaster." She fires the apple core at my waste basket.

"Ah, a perfect three-pointer," she declares with arms raised in delight.

"Good shot, Randy!" I congratulate her, and I high-five her before saying, "I know I do get stressed whenever I think I'm not living up to her standards, even though she's just a student like the rest of us. I lack confidence, I guess."

"She can be intimidating for sure, but you have mature thinking Torr, so trust in that. And on that note, what do you think about the new English prof?"

"I'll tell you what I think of her," chirps Dawn-Rae, sauntering into the room to join us. "She's a brave lady—the only female on the teaching staff! I believe we should have more ladies on staff to bring a feminine perspective and balance things out. God made male and female, you know, and we are all created equal. Hey, Torr, what's with the sweater? Seems like you're always wearing it. Do you sleep in it too?"

"Actually, yes, I do," I reply. "Only because it's Christmastime. It's a gift from Dad that last Christmas together. We each got one, just different colours; it's one way I face Christmas since his death."

"I'm glad you talk so freely about your dad, Torr," Randy says. "I wish I had known him, but I'm glad I know you, my brave friend!"

These young women have buoyed me up and meant so much to me. We all have strong opinions and varied family perspectives on things and different experiences, but we agree on the important things. God is central to our lives, love is the essence of life, and our families are our strength. This is how we'll embrace our future, wherever that may lead us on our separate paths.

Dawn-Rae interrupts my thoughts. "Hey, Torr—sleepyhead. I was just thinking about our triple-dating times at college, and especially a certain blind date trick we pulled on you! And look where that has taken you, Miss Bride Today!"

I feel a little sheepish on recalling I didn't like Serge and rejected him every time he asked me out. I had eyes for someone else. But Randy and Dawn-Rae pulled a sneaky on me with the blind date idea. (I later discovered it was going to be Serge's last try.)

I soon had eyes for him only. Both of us are sports-minded, both of us have some health issues, both of us come from small towns, and both of us are gregarious, community-minded sorts.

We both lived in northern communities too—I in Alberta and he in British Columbia. It's so strange to think we ended up meeting each other in the quaint prairie province of Saskatchewan.

Of course, it is great that he is handsome, with his laughing blue eyes; thick, curly black hair; and cleft chin. He is a talented hockey rogue, avid golfer, and good volleyball and basketball player. No wonder he gets "Athlete of the Year" awards. And he sings tenor on the college touring ensemble. Everyone loves Serge. Now I've fallen under his spell too.

"You can take credit for the matchmaking, Dawn-Rae," I concede amiably. "You and Randy both. And now Serge and I are actually getting married!"

My family labels me a romantic. They tease me about my history of infatuation with heart-throbs like Wayne Gretzky. I realize his playing career started the year I was born, but I was raised watching every Oilers game with my dad. Isn't it understandable how a young girl could fall for the Great One? I was fourteen years old when his grand wedding to American actress, Janet Jones took place in Edmonton. Sadly, we weren't invited, but Dad humoured me with a drive by the stately church the next time we were in Edmonton. And, yes, I had other equally distant loves. Mom really liked that, because she didn't have to monitor those relationships—safety in distance, you know. But there have been a few not-so-distant beaus too. Now here I am with Serge, who beat out all the competitors, just like the Great One. He should feel pretty good about that!

We chose 29 July as our day. And now that day is here—the day that will mark our commitment publicly.

How long have I been lying here daydreaming? I think I hear Randy returning from the shower.

I feel drained whenever I dream about Dad not being truly dead but just needing me to sleuth it all out and find him—rescue him. That's the good thing about dreams; you can do what you want, sort of. At least I revisit how much I miss him, though I can't make him come back. I can't find him, and he doesn't find me. He's just beyond my reach, my call, my view. There are limits to dreams too, I guess.

Well, now I'm orientated to person, place, and time, and it's time to get moving; there's so much to do to get ready.

I'm excited, but in a queasy way. Maybe I won't be able to eat the elaborate breakfast Mom is preparing for us so we can start the day with celebration and nutrition. From my jumbled thoughts, I settle on a few clear questions: Am I ready for marriage? Is he? Do I love him enough to last for always? Does he? I'm scared, but I sense fingers of courage within me somewhere.

I feel exhausted, though, and I haven't even got out of bed yet!

"Hey, get up sleepyhead," Randy admonishes me as she returns. "You can't get married by proxy, you know; you are expected to put in an appearance. And such an appearance that's going to be!" Her light-hearted banter is meant to get me laughing. "By the way, which gown are you planning to wear today?" she says, teasing me further.

My guilt over purchasing a second wedding gown raises its ugly head again.

"No girl should start her day with a gown she hates," Mom

counselled me when she found out my change of mind about the dress. "You can adjust your budget and cut corners elsewhere."

In the end, I found just what I wanted on a sale rack locally, and I was still coming in under budget; it just needed some alterations from a skilled seamstress.

Lucky for me, Mom believes a bride should create her wedding the way she dreams it, not the way the mother dreams it. The only stipulation is to live within the budget afforded.

"Funny girl, Randy," I chide back.

"This gown is even prettier than your first one, especially with you in it," lauds Randy. You are the only first-time bride I know who has two wedding gowns. Not even the Hollywood stars can boast that!" I am laughing despite my sensitivity around my squandering of wedding funds in purchasing a second gown.

Dawn-Rae struggles out of her floor nest. "How can I continue my beauty sleep with you two guffawing?"

"You've had enough beauty sleep," I respond to my gorgeous dark-eyed friend, looking so youthful with her sleep-tousled dark mane obscuring part of her smooth face but not those full rosy lips.

I'm heading for my shower, and you are next Dawn-Rae," I remind her, "and you'd better not fall back to sleep again."

In the bathroom, I sit and reread my letter to Dad before getting in the shower. I write a letter every year on his birthday, but this year he'll get this extra one, written specially to mark my marriage and wedding day. My getting married is worthy of an extra writing, I feel.

> Dear Dad,
>
> So, it's almost six years now. How can so much happen in just six years? I wonder what all has happened for you in these six years. For you there isn't a time bubble though, like us, right? If that's true, you won't be as lonely as us. We miss you every

day, at every event, with every change in our lives
without you—like this, my wedding day!

How can you not walk me down the aisle today?
You are missing out on so much, Dad! I've chosen to
have Mom escort me. But I am hoping I will sense
you walking on my other side.

I have told Serge so much about you and shown
him lots of photos, so I think he sort of knows you.
Don't forget me, Dad. I'll never forget you.
I love you,
Your blue-eyed china doll.

My eyes blur, and tears threaten to accumulate and fall unbidden.
I scrub them away angrily.

Now my usual luxurious shower is somewhat shortened, but I
linger as long as I dare.

I wonder, as hot water tries to smooth my thoughts, *What is
ahead? What is around the bend?*

*Dad, you are in a different level of existence. Can you see ahead?
Can you see around the bend?* I ask silently. *Are you happy for me?
Do you approve of Serge? Have you read my letter, and will you walk
me down the aisle unseen? Do you think I'm beautiful?* My questions
tumble over each other. *I had you for fifteen years of my life—longer
than my sisters got. I feel a little guilty for that luxury. I wonder what we
might argue about or discuss these days if you were here. You sure liked
to get me going, teasing me about societal limits on the roles of women
and challenging my liberal views.*

I hear Dad reasoning with me. "Torr, you want a man to be
strong and chivalrous, change tires, and open doors for you, but you
want to be paid equally and have hierarchical freedom. You want
to be a stay-at-home mom, but you also want a career. Essentially,

you want your cake and want to eat it too, right?" I see his raised eyebrows questioning.

"Who would want to have cake and not eat it?" I pointed out heatedly. I then continued more calmly. "I know, Dad, it sounds contradicting and unreasonable, but yes, that is what I want. Mom did it." I toss this at him slyly. Now what can he say without slamming Mom?

"Have you actually asked your mom how she feels about it, having experienced it a few years now?"

I realize, I still haven't actually asked Mom to share her experience, but I know she has assumed we'd all go to university like her. I think that's mostly because she loves school and learning, not because she has big career goals.

Dad, I guess you just liked to play the role of devil's advocate and to be a soundboard for my youthful understanding of complex issues.

Perhaps it takes many folks to replace one person's role in one's life. I acknowledge how my friends sort of play that role now. I try to imagine what Dad would be saying to me now.

As I wrap myself in the thickness of the comforting pale blue bath towel, I feel less burdened; I'm tired but full of anticipation. A deep, deep sigh escapes me, but I'm ready to celebrate this day, our special day—Serge and I with our enduring families.

Giving my locks one last vigorous towelling, I emerge from my steamy oasis to begin a truly historic day—my history, that is.

"Who used up all the hot water?" someone screams from the main bathroom as I enter the kitchen to help Mom with last-minute preparations. It sounds like N. C. I guess my somewhat shortened long shower overstressed the tank after all. Oops. Oh well, maybe I'll be forgiven quickly today because it's my wedding day.

"I had that dream again, Mom—trying to catch up to Dad in the crowds somewhere in South America," I say wistfully.

"Not surprising, I guess, this being a day of great change in your life and him not here to walk you down the aisle," she says knowingly, watching me intently. "I know how much you wanted that tradition fulfilled. Me too!"

"I promised N. C. no tears, but I don't think I will be able to do it."

We cling to each other and let the tears flow unchecked while the pain of loss seeps out of me. Maybe that is the gift of tears. They let the pain flow out and make room to receive joy. *Maybe I will manage the grand entrance tear-free*, I hope anew.

I smell fresh bread baking—cinnamon rolls is my guess.

"Mom, remember when you first went back working at the hospital in Fort Mack and tried to simplify your duties at home by doing things like no longer making homemade bread?"

This brings a laugh as she says, "Right. Your dad decided he'd take that role on and called me at work over and over, asking if it should be rising yet, etc. After the third call, I suggested he might have forgotten the yeast! Sure enough, no yeast. He threw it all out and started over. He was successful on the second batch, and I still have a photo of those six beautiful loaves. Now I'm crying again!"

I realize breakfast is ready and offer to ring the bell as a diversion.

Still caught in faraway memories, Mom continues, "I realized how much my homemade bread meant to him and added it back in to my essential home duties." We start to laugh again, but it fizzles out.

"Breakfast is ready; come and dine, my ladies all!" I call out, determined to lighten our mood as I reach for a bell to accompany my call. There are a number to choose from. I choose the tall, delicate crystal one Mom and Dad brought back from England when I was just a baby. It seems fitting for the occasion, and strangely enough, people always hear it as easily as the Swiss cowbell we use most often. Every task seems anchored in tradition. Dinnertime was always signalled by someone ringing the bell—so much nicer than bellowing all through the house or yard. We girls had no excuse for being late to the table, because we couldn't say so innocently, "Oh, I didn't hear you calling, Mom." The bell seemed to beckon rather than irritate, and we just never thought of ignoring it. *Strange how we tick*, I think to myself.

As I wait for everyone to arrive for breakfast, I quickly peek in the oven and check the evocative smells. I remove the Bundt pan and flip the contents onto the destined round glass pedestal dish. The mundane task clears my soul, and I mentally review the schedule ahead and also check the contents of the emergency case. Gina had had that idea, and the list has been revamped and double-checked many times over during this past month. It will be restocked in three weeks for N. C.'s special day. I wonder if we have missed some essential item.

My thoughts are interrupted by the sounds of feet arriving from all over the house, and I clutch Mom in another slow, desperate hug. We sit down to a prewedding feast—a feast for the wedding-party women.

There is orange juice in goblets bubbling with ginger ale, a pedestal crystal bowl heaped with fruit salad, an oven-baked omelette, slim sausages sautéed in apple juice, the reminiscent Bundt tower of cinnamon pull-aparts, and the family staple, butter to slather on the cinnamon rolls. This should nourish us for the exciting day ahead.

Somehow, we keep nearly to the schedule. Hair appointments stretch on and on and pose a few disappointments even before we get back home.

"Look at these tight curls!" Gina complains

"I think you look cute," Randy says.

"I wasn't going for cute," reprimands Gina with a sour look.

"Well, what about this updo?" N. C. says, seconding the complaints as we arrive home and she starts pulling out pins. "Can someone fix this mess?"

I think the photographer is having a hoot catching some really bizarre scenarios, and I hope she caches this one—N. C. furiously yanking pins out of her fresh do.

Note to self, I think as I swallow a smile. *If I ever get married again, don't involve a hairdressing visit.*

Now back home, I find Mom's spa friend, Suzie, ready with her make-up paraphernalia, and we bask in her artistic magic that calms us all.

Mom has always been a punctuality freak, and I know today is no exception. Each of us can relate at least one story of being left behind because we weren't ready to leave at the arranged time.

Dad didn't have the same obsession, and I chuckle while remembering one of their stories from early years of marriage. As I recall, Mom was up early to be ready for their weekend road trip. She waited and waited, making lots of noise to prod her new husband awake. Alas, no success. So she left without him. Of course, she had to turn around and wait for him; how could she possibly explain the absence of her hubby to the hosts on arrival! She later acknowledged the blessing it was that Dad could sleep so well despite noise; he did a lot of shift work and could sleep even with toddler noise about.

Still, I heave a sigh of relief when it looks like we'll be ready for the limo ride to the church.

I'm wondering how today will go. I'm hoping there will be no more surprises or disasters.

"Girls, the limo is here," Mom announces.

Everyone assists me in first, cautiously enfolding yards of train and veil to hold in my lap. I feel as if I'm in a protective chrysalis, waiting to erupt as a butterfly.

The ride to the church is marked with excited chatter. Looking out the window, I watch people on the street and at the red-light intersections and wonder what is happening in their lives today. It looks like something ordinary, while my day today is extraordinary. I feel out of place, as if I'm in a dream or in someone else's life.

"Earth to Torr," N. C. beckons me. "We're here, space girl. Let me help you untangle all that fabric and netting."

Walking on feet of clay, mouth dry and heart pounding, I arrive surrounded by my hovering entourage. They all desert me, one by one, as their particular music begins.

Now the doors close and it's just me and Mom, primed and in position for my grand entrance. I turn to Mom and take hold of her arm. We are both shaking.

The double doors are opened by the ushers, and I paste a smile on my face and look blindly down the forever aisle.

Then I see Serge smiling at me, and his confident blue eyes draw me forward. I feel Dad's blessing and approval of my maturing commitment.

I glance at Mom once more, exchange a smile with misty eyes, and walk confidently forward.

I fleetingly think of my promise to N. C., but I know this is me, and I'm going forward, embracing my future.

BOOK 3

Gina

May 2008

I am the youngest in a family of three daughters. Taking charge and getting things done is just natural for me; that trait has taken deeper roots over the years. I learned very young, and vividly, that I can't lean on someone else; they can be snatched away with no warning, leaving me bereft.

I have strong opinions and like to share them. I have no patience with manipulators or people playing mind games; I want people to just be real. Not everyone appreciates that, and I've learned to say sorry and try to keep listening; relationships are important to me.

I choose my friends carefully and commit to them once trust is grown. Apparently I have more traits of a firstborn than a youngest. Actually, I sort of sound like a hard-ass, but I have some soft spots too.

I've always known I want a good man in my life and a good marriage—a marriage like Mom and Dad had. I've always known I want children—preferably three girls, just like our family. I've known I love interior design and event planning, and I've come to know I have a green thumb.

And I'm truly a cat lady. Borneo was my solid rock when Dad died. For a cat, his life was long—at least eighteen years. That wasn't long enough.

I'm twenty-nine years old now. I married young, just before my twenty-first birthday. We enjoyed a couple of weeks in Florida for our honeymoon, both of us too young to even rent a car!

The many years of university, youthful adventures, and even that year living in faraway Petawawa, Ontario, during Stu's fourth-year work experience contract at Canadian Nuclear Lab in Chalk River was still mostly great. We've kept out of debt with his scholarships, his summer employment, and me working full-time. The teacher assistant diploma I secured along the way is totally useless but confirms I need to be the teacher, not the assistant. Tips working as a server in a restaurant offer better pay, and that's important at this stage.

But then we chose to start a family and for me to be a stay-at-home mom; debt is piling up exponentially, compounding like Canada's national debt. I hope my chosen role of motherhood pays big dividends eventually, to compensate for financial losses.

Gone are the youthful days of a dozen pair of designer jeans and elite hair salons and driving my fun deep green VW Cabriolet all over the country. A sun-lightened blond I was in those days, from driving that convertible, but also sunburned red I was a few times too! My delicate skin tones don't stand up to strong rays; that's for sure. Even the more responsible days of early marriage have faded.

Those carefree days seem so long ago. Motherhood comes with a cost, and I hope I possess the inner resources to pay the price.

And now we're heading on towards Stu's postdoctorate in Germany. So the adventure continues.

We're taxiing out to the runway. I feel detached and numb. *Did Stu and I really make this decision?* I wonder as I turn to look at him.

He looks real enough, with his long legs scrunched in the pygmy seat space; his sandy hair is freshly cut, eliminating his recent wild, woolly professor style and framing his deep-set blue eyes. He's looking back at me, and I blink like a deer in the headlights. He winks at me.

"What are you thinking, Gina?"

Still staring back at Stu, I run my hands through my straight ash-blonde hair, gaining some thinking time. My mind replays a panic attack I experienced early in our marriage. Stu had a conference in Orlando, and I joined him for the week. One night he drove to the mall to get his cherished bubbly water stash replenished. Expecting him back in half an hour, I began to panic as each half hour after that passed. I knew something terrible had happened and I was alone. I envisioned the police not knowing how to find me with the news. Thankfully, Mom answered when I phoned her in desperation dread. Talking to her settled me enough to continue the wait, knowing I could call again as often as needed till Stu returned.

He did return.

I don't even remember what had delayed him. I just appreciate that he tries really hard not to give rise to my single most glaring weakness—fear of losing him, just as Mom lost Dad.

I finally say, thinking, *At least we're together*, "This feels so very different from flying somewhere for a holiday. The number of unknowns overwhelms me. The time commitment overwhelms me. I need a more concrete word than 'adventure'."

"You're probably right. What shall we call it?" he asks, narrowing his eyes and looking thoughtful.

I'm usually very quick with my answers, observations and opinions, so I blurt out, "Insanity. Immaturity. Stupidity. Should I go on?" I challenge, with brows arched.

"No. That pretty well covers it," he agrees, nodding slightly. Our insecurity in our big decision to take on his postdoc in Germany resurfaces.

Stu grew up with one older brother, and I, two older sisters. Perhaps that influences our perspectives, but more relevant is my straightforward concrete thinking, versus his slow-burn, cerebral, scientific approach to problems. I recall asking him once, early in our dating, as he navigated the busy Deerfoot Freeway en route to our outing, "What are you thinking, Stu?" Of course, I assumed he was thinking about his lovely companion, *moi*, and the event we were going to and how much fun we'd be having.

He proceeded to explain a complex maths equation he was working out in his mind. The insight I gained that day has served me well as a key to understanding my chosen mate as being very different from me. I have other strengths, and we complement each other, but our differences create frequent tension too.

Now at this stressful time, strangely, we both have similar perspectives: both of us from Venus or both from Mars and at a standstill. At this particular crossroad, we appreciate Mom's prodding to do what needs to be done and move forward on our *chosen* path.

At least the kids are happy at the moment.

I turn and look back a couple of rows to reassure myself that Mom is indeed travelling with us. I'm grateful for that. She gives a little wave, and I smile in return. I guess this is real; I'm not dreaming. We are in the dark skies, leaving everything we know behind.

Last night was certainly real enough. There were six plastic Walmart tubs scattered over Mom's family room, and we were trying to choose carefully and pack in all our essential worldly goods.

I simply short circuited and ceased to function.

Five months ago, at the start of this decision, it seemed rational and even exciting; we felt baby Elliott was hitting a manageable stage, and our bright-eyed girl, Jewel, was well past three already. We reasoned it was a perfect time for such an adventure.

Stu's University of Alberta peers and advisors had all counselled him to jump at this opportunity as well. It was known as one of the best research labs in the world, and he'd be doing exactly what he was gifted to do—neurological MRI research.

We exited UofA student housing; stored, sold, and gifted our things; lived with family to conserve money; and awaited Stu's thesis defence.

One defence judge was from the USA, and getting his schedule to work with the local academics was a nightmare. The constant delay in setting the date for his defence was nerve-racking and made our date for moving to Germany constantly in flux. This was not a good combo for me, the organized family manager.

Finally, my last step, which I soon realized should have been step one, was making time for a four-hour-long wintry drive with my kids to the country cemetery to revisit my dad's graveside. I ponder that visit over and over.

Carrying snuggly Elliott, bundled close to me, and firmly holding my independent Jewel's mittened hand, I stumbled through the deep, deep snow. Strong winds tore at us, but bright sun tried to cheer the day and defy the -20° C January temperature.

"Mom, can I make a snow angel here, on top of Grandpa's grave, so he can see me having fun?" Jewel asked, interrupting my foggy brain and shortening my reverie.

Looking down at my spunky three-year-old, a few red tendrils escaping her Strawberry Shortcake_toque, and her happy blue eyes trusting me, I felt anew the sadness that Dad doesn't know my children. He would be proud, I know. He would add fun to their lives.

I loved her simple understanding of Grandpa watching her make a snow angel, and I smiled and said, "I think the snow is too deep today, little lady, but you can place the pine branch beside the headstone, like leaving a gift for him. How will that be?"

Placated, Jewel laid the branch, and we trudged back to the car, half frozen, while I hoped we'd be able to back out of the snowdrift I was parked in.

Though my yearly visits have sometimes grounded me in the past, this visit didn't. Reading the towering gravestone eulogy and familiar scripture yielded no comfort or direction, but only fear and sadness, as I stamped my feet in the deep snow to keep warm. Perhaps this crazy move to another continent was the barrier; the visit seemed like a fresh goodbye, and I felt that familiar tightness in my chest. I knew I needed to cry, but it was too cold, just like his burial day. Resentfully I blinked them away furiously. I hadn't been prepared for that very fresh overwhelming sense of loss.

"I will be back in two years, Dad," I promised.

I feel the plane lurch a bit and am brought back to the present. I glance at the kids, expecting them to be concerned.

They are so lucky. They are oblivious to the present dangers of flying and have no clue as to what is happening to our family; I am thankful for that.

As I sit in the endless hum of the flying beast, my mind drifts to my apprehension-fuelled paralysis of last night. I was just staring menacingly at the six tubs we were cramming with all our worldly goods to accompany us to Germany.

Glancing at Stu, I suspected he was thinking the same as me: "Let's just forget this whole idea."

Mom, however, had greater faith in us and our combined wisdom. She would prefer us to stay in Canada too, but she could see the opportunity we had seized as a blessing in our lives both now and when we would look back on our lives later. Something like that anyway.

What I do remember her sharing, and what got my attention and brought me out of my muddy fog, was her analogy of me in labour. Elliott was still only eleven months old, and his challenging delivery was still fresh in my mind and every part of my existence, so Mom's analogy resonated fully.

"Gina, this is like transition when you are in labour," she solemnly stated. "You want out of it, but there is no going back. You just accept the pain and hard work and trust in a wonderful outcome." She looked sure of herself, and we both admired her support of us in the past, so I latched onto those words and did my best to unlock my frozen self. I slowly began to focus and make the hard decisions of what to pack in those meagre tubs, and to let go of the tons of stuff I had to leave behind.

Let go indeed, I thought morosely.

Life is full of letting go of things or persons you don't want to let go of!

Last night was just another exercise in letting go.

I usually loathe flying. I'm a bit better since Mom married Bart, an airline pilot. While living at home with them for a couple of years as I went to university and worked at Montana's, I gleaned vital understanding of the particular noises and movements of an aeroplane; that has helped me somewhat, at least.

Strangely enough, I've hardly had a snippet of flying fear today. There are too many other fears taking precedence, I guess; there are so many things crowding my mind and heart for attention that getting on the aeroplane didn't faze me.

"Mom, can I have more gum, and can I have my puzzles to play with?" Jewel asks, bursting into my awakening revelation.

I answer in my teaching opportunity voice. "You can have your puzzles, but remember the gum is a special treat; you will have more when we are landing in Germany. It will protect your ears, right?"

"Ah, Mom. Please," she entreats with her puppy dog look, meant to melt my reason away.

"Oh, Gina, let her have some gum," Stu intervenes. "We brought lots, and it's a long flight. Might as well pull out all the stops and protect those little ears."

"While not protecting those little teeth?" I point out smugly, but I dole out a piece of gum reluctantly and give Stu a withering look.

I'm usually the softie, and Stu the strict one. *What's with this role reversal?* I wonder.

Elliott seems content sitting on Stu's knee at the moment. *How long will that last?* I wonder. I feel a chuckle rise in my throat as I view Stu's cramped position, holding Elliott on his knees in this sardine-can. Yeah Air Transat!

I suspect it will get worse before the nine hours are up. I'd better enjoy the chuckle of the moment. I don't think there will be many more.

Thoughts of "What are we doing?" surface again in a moment of quiet. *Are we crazy? Is there anything at the other end of this flight?* I feel as though I'm flying off to forever and for always ... nothingness. As I stare out the small, thick windowpane, I try to imagine I can look into my dad's face way up here in these dark, heavenly spaces. *Can you see me, Dad? Can you hear my thoughts?* The face looking back at me, however, merely reveals my outline of shoulder-length hair and a hazy, narrow face. My frightened blue eyes are lost in that blurry image, and there's certainly no evidence of Dad looking back at me.

To ward off paralysis as I did last night at Mom's place, I turn to focus on Jewel and play puzzles with her.

Arrival

We are actually in Germany, and we land smoothly at the mammoth Frankfurt International Airport. Yippee! With scratchy eyeballs and robotic movements, we are herded off the beast and strain to see directions for reclaiming our treasured tubs and luggage.

It is wonderfully green here, and I feel the humidity already. And we are actually standing again. I didn't think it would be possible. Well, Stu is maybe not quite standing his full height of over six feet yet. He's certainly in high gear though, getting everything done, collecting bins, and getting the rental cars.

The plan is to load one small vehicle with all the bins and load the other even smaller vehicle with me, the kids, and my mom. We will follow Stu on the famed autobahn and arrive safe and sound at the Hotel Stu stayed at last Christmas when he came for his interview in Freiburg.

There are endless problems with getting two car seats for the kids that actually work.

"Stu, did you book car seats when you booked flights?" I ask, irritated by the delay and suspecting my lack-of-attention-to-detail husband has forgotten.

"Gina, I didn't forget to book the car seats. These ones just aren't safe, and I have to accompany this guy to the other terminal to find better ones." He is matching my tired irritation.

Our plan of a two-hour daylight drive to Freiburg has slipped away, and to top it off, rain is pelting down relentlessly, as if to remind us we're not welcome here. As we wait for the agent to go to the other terminal with Stu and find different car seats, Mom recounts her flight analysis.

"Why on earth don't they turn off the cabin lights for sleeping like all other transatlantic airlines do? How did you guys manage?"

"Elliott slept on me and Jewel lay across us both somehow," I reply vaguely, not stifling an open-mouth yawn. "I got some sleep against the window, but I stayed in a position so long that my whole body was screaming. I was afraid to move and wake Elliott. Stu wasn't able to sleep at all."

It's great to have Mom help with the kids while Stu and I figure out the little hiccups of getting things settled and loaded. Three extra hours! I'm so frustrated.

The kids are doing really well, though; they are just enjoying being free and noisy, I suspect.

We ready to leave the airport in tandem, and Mom' voices her unease.

"We won't be able to follow his car in this dark, Gina. And it's still pouring rain!"

"I can do it Mom; trust me," I say, trying to reassure myself as much as her.

"Gina, it's the fast, busy autobahn. It's a crazy highway and is totally unfamiliar to you."

"I can't do anything about that, Mom," I answer with a warning in my voice.

We manage all right getting out of Frankfurt. I'm sure I am following the right taillights. Mom, from her cramped place between the car seats in the back seat, voices her scepticism one more time.

"Don't worry about following him in these conditions, Gina. Just slow down and we'll find our own way. I've been to that hotel, and I think I can find it when we get to Freiburg."

I just race along, keeping pace with the lights I hope are Stu's.

After what seems like ages, we follow those lights into a rest station, and we are rewarded with a smiling Stu crawling out of his cramped vehicle. I note Mom's ill-concealed look of shock that it was the right vehicle.

"Stu, please slow down! We can't tell which lights are yours in this darkness and rain, and at such speed. How fast are you going, anyway?" I say, my voice laced with accusation. "Our four little wheels on a board feel totally unsafe!" Jet lag and driving stress add to my *poor me* perspective.

Stu, registering surprise, agrees to go slower, and we set off again. It doesn't seem to be any slower, but I know I have to keep pace. I suspect Mom is praying and trying to distract us from the perilous state we are in, singing song after song with Jewel. Jewel is fascinated by Grandma's repertoire from her childhood and asks for another and another and another. The horrible driving conditions keep our exhausted eyes and minds alert while the singing helps calm us.

Finally, miraculously, arriving at the Hotel Lowen, in Littenwiler, on the far side of Freiburg, we collapse into bed, knowing we need to be alert again in just six hours. We then are to collect our keys to our apartment, unload our worldly goods, and return one car before a second day of charges accumulates.

"I didn't think it was possible to do this trek in tandem, but you managed it, and praise God, because I never would have found this area of the city again, or this hotel, if we had got separated," Mom splutters in thankfulness and apology.

Jewel is cozied in with grandma in the cute little wooden European bed, and Elliott is sound asleep in the baby cot as I snuggle up to Stu. We lie in silence, exhausted, with our own thoughts.

I keep seeing my reflection in the aeroplane window—shades of black and grey, no colour, staring into the abyss, trying to imagine I am closer to Dad way up there in the night sky. I fall into a deep sleep with that image and that questing thought.

Day 2

I heard much about the wonderful breakfast experience at the Hotel Lowen when Mom and Stu were over last Christmas for his Uniklinic interview. Stu could travel cheaply on Bart's employee passes as long as he was accompanied by him or my mom. They did the entire trip in four days—not something they would recommend doing again, but it saved about $10,000! That was a no-brainer, as no one had a spare $10,000. The Freiburg Uniklinic was to cover some of the travel expenses, but that is yet to be seen, and I'm quite confident they wouldn't cough up $10,000 for flight expenses. Always plan for the worst and hope for the best—someone's old adage, I think. Maybe Dad's, maybe Mom's, or maybe my own.

"Is this just how you remember it, Stu?" I ask, hoping to make conversation and maybe bring some normalcy forward.

"Yes, and I'm just as tired too." He laughs hollowly, and we all focus back on our breakfast.

The dining room décor and the tables are all in keeping with the black forest motif: heavy wooden structures, white lace in the windows, and white linens on the table. It is German breakfast buffet style too: boiled eggs wrapped in cloth in a large basket, varying breads and rolls, individual glass containers to put your butter or jams in, a couple of types of sausage, muesli, milk, and juices.

Certainly a perfect start to the day, whatever day this is, I think.

"It seems like months have gone by," I muse, and I realize I have said it out loud. I'm in a different country. I don't understand any language around me. I have no home. I'm exhausted. I look at Stu with a question in my eyes.

He shrugs and meets my eyes, silently attempting to encourage me but offering no platitudes. Perhaps there are no words to capture this sense of losing time and place and person.

Elliott babbles and grabs my hair in response. He always loves to twist his fingers in my swinging tresses. Jewel is basking in having her own mini jams and butter.

"Well, I hate to break up the party, but we need to get going and find Herr Kuhn, or whatever his name is, and get our keys," Stu states boldly, with mock cheer.

Like robots we all stand, smile, and file out, leaving Stu to determine from the waitress whether we need to do anything more to settle up. When you are illiterate and have no language, you smile a lot. That much I am learning. I feel like a walk-on in a play.

I feel tinges of cautious excitement as we arrive at the apartment complex. This is to be our next home. As planned, Mom stays in the car with the kids while Stu and I meet Mr Kuhn, the *hausmeister*, and explore the place.

It's on the second floor by Canadian description but is known as the first floor in Germany. It's monotone, sterile white. It's bright and airy with humongous floor-to-ceiling windows and doors that open to the luxuriant foliage and floral frenzy of the warm and humid outdoors. Best of all, is the all-window *wintergarten* room. I feel my spirits rise perceptively.

The floors are all industrial lino, in some shade of muted blue-green-grey. The bathroom is totally tiled, walls and floors. There are no window coverings, no light fixtures, no kitchen cabinets, no kitchen sink, no fridge, and no stove or oven.

I thought I was prepared for this. We knew it from our research of housing options, but still, it feels overwhelming to see it for real. The challenge before us is daunting. We exchange meaningful looks.

Stu manages the necessary communication with our new hausmeister, hoping he will leave and let us be on our own to grapple with our new everything.

Finally, we tour the *keller*, or storage area in the basement, which is ours as well, and now we are left alone. I'm guessing Mr Kuhn has his reservations about his new tenants too.

We stand in the wintergarten, or sunroom overlooking the

courtyard, and the *spielplatz*, or playground area, in silence, holding hands.

"What do you think?" Stu asks, breaking the silence.

Never at a loss for words or opinions, I start to reply but realize my thoughts are quite a jumble.

"Let's pray," I suggest.

While we are still holding hands, Stu voices a simple prayer of thanks and asks for strength, wisdom, and patience.

We remain a few more minutes in a gentle embrace before heading back to the vehicles to begin the day's endless chores.

We bring everyone in to see the new digs and give the kids free reign in the open, echoing place we now call home. Stu and I carry all the bins and suitcases up the many stairs, leaving the cars parked on the sidewalk. That appears to be the thing to do with vehicles. Pedestrian beware! We are learning there are no safe places for pedestrians. Vehicles seem to appear from anywhere and go anywhere.

Now inside, Jewel and Elliott are having a heyday. Concrete walls, concrete floors, and concrete ceilings, with no muffling effect from furniture and draperies, make for an unimaginable noise level. Our sleep deprivation likely augments our intake of sensory overload, and both of us prefer quieter play. But how can we deprive them of the fun they are having after so many hours being strapped and trapped?

"Jewel and Elliott, what do you think of your new home?" I ask.

"It's fun!" Jewel screeches, experimenting with her echo, and she keeps on exploring.

Elliott crawls over to me as I sit on the floor in a corner to rest after the unloading feat. He crawls into my lap and snuggles in, sucking his fingers and reaching up to twist my hair. He is content, but I know he needs to eat. That will be an innovative task. We have no dishes, no cutlery, no kitchen water source, and no cooking apparatus, and he needs more than just breast milk at this age.

Stu becomes the standing human high chair. I find our one

travel spoon and begin an offering of the cold leftover breakfast stash I had wrapped in a napkin from our hotel. Thankfully, Elliott gobbles it down with his usual groans of delight when eating. Our next meal will be at IKEA, where we hope to search out all our furniture and household supplies to set up our new home and start to fill this empty space.

"We have a couple of hours before we have to return my rental car, Gina; shall we unpack these bins before heading to IKEA?" Stu inquires.

"No. It will be easier after we have picked up mattresses and things; let's just keep going" is my tired reply.

After dropping off the one rental car, we all pile into the remaining smaller one. This is just like my life at the moment—small and cramped, going who knows where.

Within a few blocks, as we approach a quiet intersection, I yell, "Stu, watch out!"

Too late.

A blur slams into us on the passenger side, and suddenly I am fully alert, all jet lag gone. I'm terrified the children will be hurt. I think of our rental car insurance costs. I think of possible legal issues and our vulnerability. I think, *Why have we come here and taken such risks? What kind of parents are we?*

We sit shaking and speechless for what seems an eternity but is likely a split second, and I hear only Jewel: "Why did you hit that car, daddy?"

"Is anyone hurt?" Stu asks as we both turn to check on everyone.

Elliott is kicking his feet, delighted in the shake-about event.

"I'm too crammed in here to get hurt!" Mom responds from her tight spot between two big car seats, attempting a bit of humour.

"My neck hurts, Daddy," Jewel says, sounding cross.

"Didn't you see him, Stu? Didn't you hear me …?" I start to chastise while picturing my fair complexion turning red with frustration and worry.

No intersections in these quasi-residential areas are marked with yield or stop signs, and we just constantly try to look all over the place. We had already figured out that bicycles had right of way no matter what the scenario, and pedestrians had no rights. "I saw the car coming, but I was first to the intersection; I thought I had time regardless," he declares while opening his door and starting to get out to examine damages. Before closing his door with a bang, he adds in defence, "He must have been really speeding."

Three police officers, one a lady, arrive surprisingly quickly in their van. We have no German language, and they have no English! To my added horror, local people file out of shops and apartments, seemingly enjoying the spectacle as if it is their afternoon diversion from a boring errand.

So our very public, glaring introduction to being foreigners continues unabated. It becomes apparent that we'll be involved a lengthy while. I am grateful onlookers are beginning to lose interest and fade away.

Throughout the surreal experience, Jewel keeps up her mantra: "Why did you hit that car, Daddy?" No answer satisfies her; she is bewildered.

"Can I take the kids?" Mom asks. "We'll just take a walk and see if there is a play area or shop nearby."

"Oh, please do," I say with relief, air rushing out of my lungs; I hadn't realized I was holding my breath. As my shoulders slump and relax a little, I suspect she senses the friction between Stu and me.

"This looks like a long process, and Jewel needs a diversion for sure. I'll get the stroller out of the trunk for you—if the police allow me," I say in disgust.

An hour and a half later, we are still shaken but are almost free again to continue our day.

As Stu is leaning over the *polizei* vehicle, signing a couple more papers, Mom ventures to ask me, "What's the damages, hon?" She sounds breezy and nonchalant, managing a sprightly smile, but I can tell she knows we want to maintain a low key and minimize the stress on the kids. I'm hoping Jewel will stop her questioning of Stu. I think she is trying to make sense of what has happened, and I don't want her to be fearful of riding in a car now.

After waiting till Jewel turns to push her little brother down the sidewalk in the stroller, I quietly explain, "We have fines of six hundred euros and"—I stop to swallow noisily—"and no cash to pay." Our saving grace is that Stu could prove he is employed at the Uniklinic. In a conspiratorial whisper, I confess in her ear, "We do have some cash, but it is for this month's rent, etc., not to be used for this right now."

Finally, the polizei all say "Ade" and drive away.

"Auf Wiedersehen," we respond feebly, and we head off to IKEA, unsuspecting of the problem awaiting us there.

We learn too late that Germany is a cash society; credit cards are rarely used or accepted there. The plan for Mom to simply use her Visa to cover the entire frugal furnishing of our home, while we'd pay her back when we moved back to Canada, looks doomed. Now with everything loaded on carts, and some ready for delivery tomorrow, we have no way to pay and no language for negotiating. By some miracle, thank you God, special permission is granted to us, the ignorant immigrants. Mom is allowed to use her card and save the day. Hallelujah, amen!

We load the family stroller to maximum strain and carry the rest, also to maximum strain—the essential items for tonight's survival of indoor camping. We manage to make it back to our apartment without loss of life or child or sanity. Actually, I must confess our sanity is in question. We lug everything up the two flights of stairs and set up camp.

"Stu, how is the European crib turning out?" I risk asking. There is a small storage room about four feet by seven feet, and we have decided to make that the nursery. The crib will fit at the back wall. I'm hopeful there is room for the rocker Stu has to build next to complete the essentials! Luckily the door opens outward. I have fun ideas already forming in my mind to make it a cute place for my cuddly little guy.

"I think it is coming together—almost done. I don't see any leftover parts, so that is a good sign," he informs me with a sly smirk.

"Wonderful. That will make tonight work better for all of us. Elliott needs his own space; I feel bad there is no window, but we must remember to always leave the door open when we head to bed. Mom, have you found the bin with the bedding?"

"Most of it, I think. Did you bring Elliott's bedding from home? I haven't found anything like that yet—just quilts for your bed and for Jewel."

"Yeah, I know it's in the bins somewhere. It will turn up," I encourage her and myself.

Once we have our indoor campsite completed, we all walk back to the Lidl store on the corner and buy some food supplies. I stand in the queue while Stu and Mom herd the kids back outside.

What an experience awaits me.

Everything goes flying by the cashier, who's sitting mutely behind the counter like a robotic machine, exhibiting speed and precision like I've never witnessed. I'm trying to get everything onto the conveyer while needing to get everything into our green grocery bags just as fast, but not succeeding. The robot is looking at me as if I'm from Mars, eyebrows raised in fixed position, awaiting payment. Do I hear her tapping her toe in impatience? I don't even look back, to see how the folks in the queue are processing this. *How did I think I could manage a simple task like purchasing a few groceries?* I berate myself. *Can anything be simple and knowable here?* I wonder, feeling my anger surge and my confidence in living here dip even lower.

I see we need to devise some system to make this work in the future. My only plan at the moment is to pawn the task of grocery shopping off on Stu. I snort derisively to myself, stuff the unknown change into my pocket, raise my chin, and march out as if unperturbed.

Finally arriving outside with my few purchases, fit in three bags,

I loudly declare, "I'm not going through that again. You can try next time, Stu, or come bag while I load the conveyer. It was a crazy and embarrassing ordeal."

"Well, sure," he says, sounding surprised. "Let's do it together next time, Gina. We'll figure out a method." This is his unsuccessful attempt to calm me.

With our few cloth bags full of supplies, we all walk on a little further to check out the inviting smells coming from the *Backerei*. We buy one loaf of *Monat Brot* and six delicious-looking buns. There is a little slot near the counter with candies for the kids. Jewel questions me with her eyes, and I nod permission, thankful Elliott is young enough to miss out. Then, on our walk back to our apartment, we decide to get brave and check out the *Metzgerei* too. The deli meats are beautifully displayed, and the regular meats look so fresh; maybe they are out of our price range, but they are definitely a great resource for a special occasion. To the kids' delight, the server offers them each a slice of bologna. Back out in the paved area again, a car brakes and honks, reminding us how difficult it is to discern where it is safe to walk; pedestrians seemingly have no rights. Keeping alert is the name of the game; I make note of this. I'm so tired I feel like a wind-up toy that's almost unwound.

Our supper of fresh bread, meat, cheese, and finger veggies is delicious, and we indulge ourselves with a treat—choco balls yogurt.

A bit refreshed, I say, "I'm so looking forward to the delivery tomorrow—particularly that little European fridge."

"Yes, and all we have to do is plug it in!" Stu says, knowing the countertop and accompanying oven, cupboards, and sinks will need constructing and special hook-ups.

Giving a returning smile, I say, "I have faith in you, my Lego guy; you can build anything. I'm going to nurse Elliott; I'm sure we are all ready for our *mats.*"

While enjoying this special time rocking and singing Elliott to sleep, I hear Stu playing with Jewel and getting her ready for bed.

I don't hear any sound from Mom and suspect she has turned in already.

Joining Stu on our floor mattress, I say, "So here we are. Day two of our adventure. Have you started our blog?"

"I took a few minutes just after Jewel quit asking, 'Why did you hit that car, Daddy?' and finally nodded off," he says, mimicking her mantra and swinging his head back and forth. "I put some pictures up, and descriptive words, like 'idiots', 'rain', 'car wreck', 'rain', 'more debt', 'rain', 'jet lag', 'rain', and 'grocery nightmare'. How's that for a start?"

"I've heard it said that honesty is the best policy, so I guess you done good, honey bear," I say affectionately in a sleepy slur.

Day 3

It's early. A happy sun is shining, and we all slept well; "Thank you God," I breathe in prayer.

But by early afternoon we all want to go back to bed. Well, the kids don't seem as affected by the eight-hour time change. Mom succumbed a couple of times, I think. I nod off while Stu is gone to find a hardware store and get an electric drill for attaching cupboards to concrete walls. Now starts the noise! With all walls being thick concrete and our cheap drill whining and vibrating, the drilling goes on nearly nonstop, hour after hour, with very slow progress.

"Stu, is that a knock at the door?" We all fall silent and wait. Sure enough, we hear another knock—more insistent, it seems, this time.

Stu and I lock eyes and shake our heads simultaneously, neither willing to face a stranger, plus knowing a language barrier is guaranteed. None of us have a word of German in our brains except "*Nein*." Oh, and "*Bitte*" and "*Danke*". Now where is that German–English dictionary when we need it?

Mom sees our hesitation, guesses our plan to ignore the obvious, and valiantly takes the challenge. She opens the door to find a tall, anorexic, smoker-wrinkled, quasi-blonde lady spewing anger at her in the guttural German, which is so perfect for showing distain. Mom listens and then points to her watch, inferring that the offence committed is possibly related to the time of day, and she apologizes in English. That seems to deescalate the situation, and our visitor turns abruptly with a huff and leaves. Our small hope that it might be a neighbour with a friendly welcome, and maybe a home-baked pie, has evaporated, and we realize it is ten o'clock at night. In our desperation to accomplish as much as possible, we have lost track of how late it is. We have no language skills to apologize and just hope that being quiet as mice now will set things right. We don't want to make enemies on our second day here. We had just learned an unspoken rule of this apartment life.

We survey our progress and Mom and I congratulate Stu on what he has accomplished. There is now one kitchen counter and a sink, though no plumbing is in place yet. We'll just continue to get our water from the bathroom sink for now. The small fridge is plugged in and working and full of edibles from our earlier shopping.

After a night of menacing nightmares intersecting my sleep, in mumble-jumble, I wake to reality and find we are indeed transplanted in new soil. Will we thrive and grow? Will we fade a sickly colour and limply strive towards the sun? Will we choke right out?

I look around our indoor camping space and see Jewel has snuggled in with Grandma, still sleeping, and I hear Elliott giggling in the storage room to Stu's morning entertaining antics. I struggle up out of our floor bed and quilts, feeling stiff and sore all over. *Is this what getting old feels like?* I wonder. This is what day one after a car-tangled intersection feels like, plus jet lag and sleeping on the floor. *I need to rally, and I need to help get on with the day's tasks*, I tell myself firmly.

May 2009

We have a routine now, born of survival skills for the immigrant, I think. Our home is truly our safety zone. Work is Stu's world, and he enjoys it; he's confident he'll get the three-year project done in two years. Hallelujah! *Only one more year to endure*, I rejoice. I press Stu continually to reassure me about this.

He has a bike for the five-mile ride to his work; otherwise, we walk everywhere.

Every day is laundry day, and our apartment is continually strung with it; we have no clothes dryer, and Germany's high humidity is my laundry's worthy foe.

Thinking back on my gardening metaphor I felt when we settled here a year ago, I assess our situation and conclude we haven't choked right out, but we aren't exactly thriving either. *I guess we're a sickly yellow but still yearning towards the sunshine*, I think, with a wicked smile.

"Gina, let's celebrate!" I hear Stu holler, and as I turn, I see him making a ridiculous face at me from the living room where he is playing with the kids. I think that is one of the specialties of dads; they know how to play. Often as I watch him with the kids, I imagine my own dad at play with me and my sisters: living room floor wrestling; the long, bumpy ride to the chicken house, riding atop the bean plants, all of us crammed in the wheelbarrow, when we lived on the acreage; riding in the dune buggy on hilly trails to the river; and, of course, the to-the-death water fights when we were camping.

What is Stu talking about celebrating, though? I wonder. As he comes into the kitchen, Jewel on his back and dragging Elliott monkeyed around his leg, he places his hands on my shoulders and continues to look at me mutely with a question in his puppy dog eyes.

"What are you talking about?" I ask, trying to hide my irritation at the interruption of my preparations for supper. I know it isn't any birthday or anniversary or statutory holiday—none known to me, anyway.

"Well, Gina, I think our surviving here a whole year bears celebrating!" Now that gets my attention. I drop my busyness for supper and stare back at him.

"You got that right buster," I concede. "Let's see now; you first, Stu."

"Well, for starters, like Jewel said a year ago, 'Daddy, you are building our home!' She was impressed, so I guess I can be too. Also, we've learned how to navigate the speedy check out at Lidl; just throw everything back in the cart, throw money at the cashier, push your cart out of the way, and then bag your groceries out of everyone's way." Stu's demo of the system while explaining it gets me laughing.

"We've learned enough language to manage basic social interactions," I say with pride. "And I have *relearned* how to make meals and bake using German systems and ingredients; I haven't had to throw anything out now for quite a few months, I might add."

As the recounting of scenarios continue, we are crying from laughing so hard. Making sure Jewel isn't listening, I remind Stu, "Maybe the worst was Jewel coming home crying from preschool last December because St Nicholas hadn't come by her house and filled her shoes like all the other kids'. We had some reasonable explanation, remember?"

"Yes," Stu replied. "Didn't we say that because we were Canadians living in Germany, St. Nicholas planned to come to our house the following day and we had her put her shoes out that night? We'll get that one right this coming December, I think."

"We'd better get it right this time—no excuse. I'm really glad we've found the church we go to, too."

Being near the university, it caters to students learning English. Some singing is in English and some in German, and the sermon has a translator. Well, we are not Germans practising our English, but it works in reverse for us—Anglophones practising our German!

"I think your idea is great, Stu. We do need to celebrate somehow. I wish we could go to Berlin for a couple of days." I wistfully throw out the idea.

"Ah, Gina, I wish we could too. I know how badly you want to make that trip."

Being realistic, and trying to minimize my strange and constant urge for visiting Berlin, I temper my suggestion: "Maybe I could make a special 'eat in' dinner next week for the two of us after the kids are in bed. It might even work to go out one evening if we wait till Mom is visiting again."

Being reminded that Mom plans to visit in a couple of weeks, Stu panics.

"That's right, Gina. I forgot about that. I will need to put the tire back on her bike. I am using it on my bike, remember? We need to budget for a new inner tube for my tire. Can the grocery budget manage that before your mom arrives? It sure is handy having her bike around for spare parts when she isn't here, but now I have to "pay the piper.""

"Funds are tight, Stu," I answer. We'll have to steal from the grocery budget for sure. Being reminded of our meagre financial situation, I feel its weight cloud my mind, and I press my lips together harshly to keep from voicing my complaint and fear.

2 January 2010

It's almost two years since we've moved to Germany. I again assess our situation using the garden metaphor. Well, we're still not thriving, but we haven't choked right out either; we're not as sickly as a year ago but still straining towards the sun. We've even managed a bit of exploratory travel when our parents have visited, but so far, we haven't made it to Berlin, despite my longings. Stu has been there for meetings, but I really want to experience it myself. It is a quest of mine. I feel driven. It calls me.

Stu's contract here was for three years, but our plan was to complete the work in two years and return to Canada with great fodder for his CV. Stu is a focused person, and that plan was reasonable and on schedule too, but things changed.

That change we've named Anika! Adding a pregnancy to our time here has necessitated a return to the original time commitment of three years. I wonder uneasily if that might turn into even longer. I suspect, too, that my chances of getting to Berlin have been further delayed.

And now here I am, still in a motherhood daze, returning to our apartment—our second one by only one week's time—and carrying our new-born daughter, delivered just a few hours ago at the Marienrhien Geburtshaus.

Mom looks shocked to see us. She left us there just three hours ago to return to the apartment and relieve our sitter, fully expecting Stu and me to stay overnight at the birthing house with our new bundle and recuperate a bit in the care of the midwife.

"What are you guys doing here? All that walking to the bus and … catching trams and … you likely haemorrhaging and … weak after that difficult delivery …" Mom sputters accusingly as we arrive home unexpectedly.

"I know, Mom," I say as I half fall through the door, "but we just couldn't fathom staying there another moment with that inhospitable, overbearing midwife while she complained to us about cost of supplies and missing holiday time with her family. So we chose not to spend any longer in her presence. In fact, if we never have to see her again, that will be even better."

"Ah, I understand. Here, let me take your little bundle and have another look at this darling," Mom says, recovering gracefully. "Anika's had a rough day too, you know, but she's sure content at the moment."

You guys settle in, and I'll make you something to eat if you'd like. The kids are sound asleep. Will they be surprised in the morning!"

Basking in some family caring and homecoming, I feel a bit encouraged despite my jittery legs and queasy stomach.

Looking around our new apartment, I feel relieved Anika had delayed making an entrance into the world. Feeling as weak as I do right now, I can't imagine having to tackle a household move. It was definitely best it was accomplished before her birth, despite my plans otherwise.

I look out our living room window and appreciate again the big, though public, yard full of fruit trees and lush privacy hedges. I know we are going to enjoy the two small concrete patios that are ours too. Like our first apartment, it borders the *spielplatz*. But now being ground floor, the kids can go right from our kitchen patio door.

The decision to move has been a hard one. We truly don't know how much longer we'll be in Germany. Six months? A year? Forever? It all depends on finding employment back home. I know Stu is doing all he can to complete his project, and he fires off his CV every chance he gets. So I say sternly to myself, "Reign in your homesickness, Gina, and focus on recovering from this birthing trauma of today!"

I know one big plus of our move to this apartment is that we will not miss our nemesis, the tall, anorexic, smoker-wrinkled, anger-driven neighbour that visited us the night we moved into our first apartment. She will have to find someone else to bully.

As I nestle into our one comfy chair, the green wicker rocker, I hold on to the delightful knowledge that Stu has two weeks off work—common practice during German Christmas scheduling. There are some nice standard occurrences like that here. Maybe I will feel strong enough by then to mother three little ones, despite feeling like an orphan myself.

April

"Stu, you won't believe what happened today on our way to the physiotherapist," I blubber incoherently into my mobile phone. "A wheel came off the stroller, our trusty Phil and Ted, in the last block before the professional building. But we managed to get there on time! The kids were so good and helpful, but I didn't think we could possibly make it back home again." My words tumbled over each other.

"Gina, slow down. Take a deep breath. Where are you now?" Stu asks.

"In our apartment. Somehow we made it back home, all four of us, but I can't quit shaking. I asked the kids to sit on their beds with their books, and I put Anika in her cot and closed the door. She's still crying, Stu. Can you come home a bit earlier today? I feel like I am going over the edge. I just want to scream and scream and scream forever. I can't do this any more, Stu."

"I can leave right away. It should only take me half an hour. The kids will be fine, Gina. Just have a glass of water and put some music on or phone your mom to talk to till I get home. She won't mind that it is five in the morning over there."

I choke out, "OK, Stu."

I do take a glass of water. I sit in the green wicker rocker, picturing Mom bearing it home our first summer, turned upside down over her head. She had seen an outdoor garage sale event near the library. Sitting in it now calms me. I don't phone her. I sit and wait for Stu.

These last four months of me twice daily treating Anika's hip dysplasia with tortuous physio, her heart-wrenching screams, and the frequent orthopaedic appointments all over the city have worn me down to collapse. Amazingly, no one has reported us for suspected child abuse!

I hear his key turn in the lock, but I can't manage to get up to meet him at the door. On some level I know I should feel embarrassed for my weakness, but I can't muster it.

Jewel and Elliott crack open their door at the sound of Daddy's voice and peer at me as I sit rooted in the chair.

"Just play in your room a bit longer, guys, and try to give Anika her soother again," Stu tells them. "I will come see you in a few minutes."

"Is Mommy all right?" Jewel asks quietly.

"Mommy is just tired, sweetheart. I will come see you in a minute," Stu assures again.

Kneeling in front of me with obvious concern in his eyes, he takes my hands in his and massages them. His warmth and silence seem to tether me again. Then I fall into his embrace and quietly cry till there are no more tears. He guides me to our bedroom, tucks me into bed, and quietly leaves to tend to the children. I register their sweet voices in the background and fall asleep once Stu has calmed Anika's crying.

When I wake a few hours later, Anika is lying beside me, wanting to nurse. Her big blue eyes smile up at me, and I feel freshly forgiven. Stu is standing there with a silent, questioning look.

"Thanks, honey bear, it's OK. I can nurse her. I'm alert and somewhat sane again. I guess the stress needs to bubble out once in a while."

"I know the feeling well, Gina. No need to apologize to me; that's for sure," he says, and he sinks down beside me with a big sigh. "I think my mindless evening run and cycling five miles to work each day gives me an outlet."

"I love you, Stu."

Placing my slim hand in his strong one, I say, "Are we going to survive this adventure? I know we're committed to at least one more year, right?" While meeting his eyes, I admit, "I'm just homesick, so homesick."

A few more tears find their way onto the pillow before I ask, "Are Jewel and Elliott OK?"

"They are fine. They're both asleep now. We all went to Lidl and picked up the forbidden yogurt with choco balls," he says, looking sheepish, "and I shared some fizzy water with them. I let them see that you were sleeping, and they didn't worry any more."

Stu crawls in beside us, and we all fall asleep.

Light has found its way into our room. Anika is not beside me; nor is Stu. I recognize sounds of breakfast and hear young chatter. It's morning. Morning has found me. I stay still, enjoying having the bed all to myself.

Stu peeks in to say, "I'm walking the kids to school. I made Jewel's lunch, and Elliott helped pack his snacks."

I nod and offer a small smile. What a treat this is.

I turn on my other side, and my eyes land on the children's art posted on our desk, and I smile more broadly. I tentatively admit I feel refreshed. A meltdown and a night's sleep seem to have been the good medicine I needed.

Returning a half hour later, Stu asks hesitantly, "Will you be fine to get Elliott from his class and walk him home later, Gina?"

I swing my legs out and sit on the edge of the bed, run my fingers through my tangled hair, and look up at him. "I believe so, my gallant knight. Thanks again, so much. I will try to be an adult for the rest of the day. How are you doing?"

"I'm doing OK, just the usual frustrations at work," he admits with an audible intake of breath and twisted smirk. I recall his recent mention of a co-worker always trying to borrow his research data rather than doing his own calculations, and the overload of colleagues asking him to edit their final copies for publication in English.

"I am worried about you, though. Our life here is a pressure cooker, I know; far away from family and friends and familiarity," I hear him say. "I'd better head down to the *keller* and fix the wheel on the stroller before I head to work. Hey, how *did* you get home with a broken stroller and three kids and such a lengthy distance?" He tilts his head down, with furrowed brow and narrowed eyes.

I give a snort as I recall the fiasco, and the whole mess pours out of me. "I kept Anika in the stroller, and I threatened Elliott with an evening sitting in his bed if he didn't hang onto the one side continually. Jewel and I lifted the broken side best we could, to keep rolling crookedly along, some of the time, and sometimes just plain dragging it." I use hand motions to demonstrate the craziness.

"How on earth did you manage the bus and tram portions?"

"Thankfully some strangers helped me lift it on," I say, shaking my head slowly. "Of course, Anika was screaming most of the way; she is never happy after her physio appointments. We were a sight to behold. Worthy of a *Funniest Home Videos* entry for sure." I again severely push my bed-head hair off my face. More calmly, I say, "Jewel was a big help, and Elliott actually did as I asked. I think it was scary for them both. I reviewed what they should do if they got left at a stop in all the chaos—just stay at the stop and wait till I come back from the next one and get them. They know the drill and remember watching it happen to a kid one time, so it didn't take much to get their attention. I just reminded them it takes a long time. I was seriously praying we could avoid that disaster at least, and people around us certainly tried to be helpful. Maybe some of them were angels sent to help this crazed mother." After a pause for effect, I say with conviction, "We are just so vulnerable here, and I can't prevent crazy things from happening. I feel threatening tears and again ask, are we going to make it, Stu?" I look at him fully with unmasked fear.

Stu, who has been listening intently through my story, says with equal conviction, "Yeah, we are. We are a team, Gina. You could be right, that angels helped you too. I'm proud of you for holding this family together day to day. You know, you are free to fall apart occasionally. You can't be tough and strong all the time. We need to find ways for you to de-stress too."

"Yeah. As if. What would those be, I wonder?" Feeling a familiar weight descend on me, I add, trying not to sound accusatory, "At least you were here, not on another continent at some conference or other."

His travelling a few times each year for seminars and meetings and to various countries for conferences remains challenging for me; I dread the fear of him possibly never returning to us.

Just like Dad.

I give a shudder and turn away abruptly, attempting to rein in my panicky thoughts.

Two Weeks Later

Our day-to-day plodding seems to be in sync again. And I have found my de-stressor! I've carved out a spot for my survival, and I think it is making a difference. Mom calls it 'care for the caregiver'. Each day I take a warm, deep half-hour de-stressing bath. Despite the open-door policy to accommodate little people, they are learning to enter only if it's an emergency. The shower curtain is my backup, and there is no talking allowed. At least I don't answer unless I deem it an emergency.

Another bright spot on the near horizon is an upcoming visit from Torr and Serge. As a schoolteacher, Serge will have Easter break, and Torr can simply close up her shop briefly. *Now if N. C. and Garrett were coming too, we sisters could have a* real *reunion, like old times*, I think longingly. I then laugh as I picture two more houseguests in our postage stamp living quarters. I feel a giggle bubble up inside as I wonder what they will think of our six-hundred-square-foot two-bedroom apartment with one bathroom!

This is the first holiday with my sister in a long time. I truly need a sister time visit. I wish just the two of us could somehow play hooky and go off to Berlin together. Where do such irrational thoughts come from, I wonder?

I think the last time we had a travel holiday together was our adventure to Nicaragua, delivering World Vision shoe boxes to orphanages and isolated communities in the Cordillera Mountains. Torr was already married, but I wasn't.

Well, one thing I know is that Torr is going to get an eyeful on this holiday spent together as well.

Hearing Stu at the door, bringing in the fresh supper fixings, I call out, "Hey Stu, how do you think Serge and Torr will adjust to our way of life here? The hardships are less oppressive than the time Torr and I spent in Nicaragua, but still so different from Canada."

"You'll be a better judge of that, Gina," he responds as he places fresh crusty rolls, salami, pepperoni, hot peppered cheese slices, and butter on the table.

As I add fresh veggies and my home-made jams, I reiterate my comparisons.

"It will be a friendlier climate this time of year, and no howling, incessant Nicaraguan winds. We can provide a three-piece bath with an open-door policy for the nine of us while they are here, and hey, that's certainly a step up from a makeshift outdoor latrine!" I say, giving an elegant, sweeping bow and pointing towards the bathroom. Stu nods and fakes an impressed, surprise, eyes agog and hand pressed over his open mouth. Enjoying his response, I continue. "The language barrier will be German rather than Spanish, and the tour guides, you and moi, will be helpful and friendly, but maybe less informed, as we have only lived here two years and are still working on language!" Suddenly I stop. The reality of easy communication hits me square on, and I brighten, exclaiming, "Am I ever going to enjoy the ease and comfort of speaking in English; maybe I will be talking non-stop the entire visit. And being understood. And understanding them. And discussing important things. I can hardly wait, Stu!" I then return to our galley kitchen to get a jug of milk and call out to Jewel and Elliott playing on the patio, "Kinder zum tisch, bitte."

Later in the evening, thinking of us being tour guides in a couple of weeks, I interrupt Stu's reading of a bedtime storybook to Jewel and Elliott.

"Stu, what do you think of renting a vehicle when Torr and Serge are here and maybe doing a day through the Alsace wine route, and even a little stop in Colmar?"

Everyone loves Colmar, France, which is only an hour away by car and is known as Little Italy because of its canal system.

"We'd take Anika with us, but Mom and Bart would watch these cherubs, I know."

"Are we cherubs, Dad?" inquires Jewel.

"We not shrubs, Dad," mimics Elliott scornfully and with authority.

"Cherubs are like young angels, and yes, you are definitely cherubs—my cherubs." He begins tickling them, to squeals of delight.

I heave a big, noisy sigh, admitting my interruption has been counterproductive for settling the kids for bedtime.

Minutes later, Stu emerges from the kids' room, and we continue our discussion about the upcoming visitors expected and what sightseeing we could fit into the week.

"Stu, did you know Zoe and Oliver are heading home to Australia for a couple of months? I bet they'd be totally fine to have Mom and Bart use their apartment. During the day, they'll be watching our *cherubs*, but there's no room for sleeping here," I reason aloud.

Zoe and Oliver, our tall, blonde, hippy-type Australian friends, are opera singers on contract here for a few years. We know them from church, and they are our only English-speaking friends. *How I envy them and their frequent flights back to their own country*. I think, *spoiled brats*. I wish I were a similar spoiled brat with the luxury of flying home every few months. Trying to push my dark thoughts aside, I ask, "Are all three in there asleep, Stu?"

"Yes, I think their apartment for Mom and Bart is a good idea, and yes, the girls are sleeping, but Elliott is still awake and reading his books. I think I even dozed off."

Suddenly I'm struck with a troubling thought. With hands on hips and my chin raised, I say, "Everyone loves to come here and visit. They have a great time and tell us how lucky we are. And we hate it here. What's wrong with us? What's wrong with me?"

Stu offers no quick answer, so I storm on. "We've put in our two years here but see no end in sight. We're second-class citizens here. I'm not allowed to work. We can't afford heat in the winter or independent travel to the many alluring and historical places so near us." Then, raising my voice, I add, "Unless our parents foot the bill. How sad is that?" I continue pacing the tiny square that is our living room. "I wish we could treat them once in a while!"

"I don't think they mind, Gina," Stu reasons.

I turn abruptly, almost slamming into him, and hiss, "That's not the point at all! When will we ever get our heads above water? When will we come close to our big dreams? When will you be done with your project and have a decent job?"

Feeling spent, I plunk down on the living room daybed, guest bed, laundry rack, play space, reading nook and tuck my legs up under me. I grab the two cheery, giant pillows tightly to my chest in frustration, and rest my head on my crossed hands.

After a lengthy space of silence, Stu says, "I think I will go for my run."

Left alone with my thoughts, I finally rise and creep into the kids' room; peace and quiet and tiny wisps of breathing greet me. I have three beautiful, unfathomable little creatures, trusting and whole, and I have Stu, my faithful partner. I truly am blessed. I need to rest in that and let the fretting go, I know.

Reaching up to place my hand on Elliott's warm blonde head, so near the bunk slats, I ask God to protect him in this harsh German setting. I gently slip his glasses off, noting afresh the repairs they need and the lack of money to do it. Turning to the other bed, I trip over a toy that starts singing happily in German. Holding my breath and standing as still as a statue, I wait till I'm sure no one wakes.

Letting my breath out in relief, I bend and reach down to adjust covers over Jewel, thinking she is her name. *What a precious jewel she is to me. God, please continue to grow her spirit of joy in living.*

Finally, in the soft light of the room, I carefully walk over to Anika's nook. The portal window above her Euro-crib allows an angelic aura to settle gently over her, taking my focus off her trussed-up position in her ever-present hip dysplasia brace. I can't avoid noting her persistent frown, even in sleep. My heart hurts for her anew. But the light, like a rainbow after rain, offers me a promise of God's care of her, and I feel God's peace. *God, give me strength, love, and wisdom to care for those entrusted to me*, I pray.

I hear the apartment door open and know Stu is safely home. I meet him there and smile at his soggy appearance; his glasses are fogged, his clothes and hair dripping.

"You're a sight, my Neanderthal!" I greet him

Peering over his foggy specs, he nods and smiles while heaving breathlessly from his run. He then carefully removes his wet outerwear.

"You need new runners, Stu," I say, staring menacingly at them. "Your feet must be soaked with those holey things".

"Soon, I hope, but Elliott needs new glasses first and foremost."

"You are right," I agree with a sigh. "I managed to get them off without the arm breaking again when I peeked in on him just now, but I wonder how long we can limp this one along. Hey, thanks for absorbing my rant of frustration earlier tonight, Stu." I reach up to embrace my still half-drenched, co-adventuring anchor.

I feel his muscles relax, and looking up, I see a gentle smile crack his rugged five-o'clock-shadow face.

After a change into dry clothes, Stu joins me in the kitchen, grabs a cup of his special formula gut-destroyer coffee brew and says in reference to our earlier discussion, "Gina, I did some thinking about your suggestion, and I think a car rental for one day that would allow us to do the wine valley touring is a great idea. I will start looking into the costs for a small car that can accommodate a baby seat too.

"That sounds great, Stu," I say as I return to the kitchen and the baking needed tomorrow for the kids' classes. I mentally list the places we'd like to visit while Torr and Serge are here. The *Minsterplatz* is a must see, including the *Minster* with its majestic Romanesque and Gothic architecture, plus the magnificent bell tower with Germany's oldest Angelus bells. The first time I experienced it, I was navigating a stroller and two kids. As I broke free of the store-lined cobbled street, it suddenly overshadowed my path, and I couldn't breathe; it was so majestic! *Perhaps it is what arrival in heaven will be like*, I muse. I hope I can spring it on Torr in a similar fashion and watch her reaction.

Of course, we'll take the short train ride up the Hochfirst mountain to Titisee, where there is a great cuckoo clock shop, pretty parks, and Schwartzwalder decor throughout the town, as well as a restaurant with traditional German dining, served family style, and quite affordable. If we don't do that, we certainly will make a stop at a *backerei* or two for individual delicacies to enjoy on the ride back down the mountain.

We'll ensure they have a Lidl grocery store experience, and of course Mom and us girls will hit the wonderful tea houses to introduce them to my favourite delicacy of *apfelstrudel mit vanillesosse*!

A road trip to Berlin, distant and expensive, will have to wait, I know.

August 2011

I've had time to ponder Torr's bit of information when they visited over a year ago, and I mull it over constantly.

On a sunshiny restaurant patio in Colmar, amidst baskets of colourful flowers, French chatter, and the rippling creek sounds, she had leaned forward excitedly, and said, "Gina, I think I might know why you are fixated on getting to Berlin." After waiting only briefly for my reaction of alert surprise, she continued. "I think there is a connection with Dad's death. You were only eleven and might not remember a creative discussion we girls had with Dad just a couple of weeks before the accident. Or your mind might deliberately be blocking that memory."

Sitting up straighter, I laid my fork aside, forgetting my anticipation of the savoury crêpe before me. "How mysterious, Torr. What conversation are you referring to?" I asked tentatively while searching my mind for something about Berlin in my childhood.

"Well, it might have nothing to do with anything, but I had brought up the fact that in my social studies class, our teacher had spent quite a bit of time on the exciting news that the Berlin wall had suddenly been opened up and later totally demolished after thirty years of immobilizing and separating families and business. That happened in November 1989, just a few weeks before Dad's accident."

I frowned and leaned back in my chair with arms crossed loosely, wondering where this was going, and I said pointedly, "Go on."

"He challenged us to consider what that would be like if Fort Mack suddenly enacted a similar edict. We had a lot of fun imagining things of convenience, such as missing maths class because our school was on the other side of the river—the natural barrier. But soon we envisioned the possibility of being separated from one of our parents, or even both, if we kids were on one side for an event and Mom and Dad were at home on the other side. Because it's something that happened around the time of Dad's death, it could easily be bundled in with all the sadness and changes and lost memories."

I sat in stunned silence, drinking up her words, my eyes never leaving her face.

"Perhaps," she further posed, with arched brows and wide smile, "visiting Berlin, now enveloped in freedom, will have some effect on you or your memories."

I am still determined to get to Berlin and view the site of the Iron Curtain, but having this titbit of possible connection in my psyche strangely fills me with caution. I think I fear finding out it won't help me remember.

My reverie ends abruptly with an excited seven-year-old rushing me. "Mom, can I take something special from Germany for Langston when we all visit Canada?"

Our upcoming trip is especially exciting for her. She remembers everything about her life before Germany. Now she is daily spouting her stories from when she lived in Canada.

Soon we will all see everyone and get a good, long visit. I'm so excited I, too, can hardly sleep or eat! Stu has been back home once for his PhD graduation and once en route to Hawaii for a conference, but the rest of us have never been back.

Our parents are gifting us this trip. Excitement is high, even though Elliott and Anika don't even know what "Canada" means and Elliott has a leg cast from an injury in the playground last week. We leave next Tuesday and will be gone a whole month.

What will it be like? I wonder. *Will it seem normal or foreign? Will I feel more connected to Dad back in Canada? Will I feel reverse culture shock, like the time I returned from Nicaragua? I've been away three years now, and I feel settled here, but am I?*

Canada

I am almost home. I peer out the small window and get a glimpse of the Calgary International runway beneath me. I'm tired. We're all tired. Elliott has vomited twice. The reliable westerly wind coming over the Rockies with nothing to stop it but us is buffeting us, but nothing deters my bubbling joy.

I reach for Stu's hand as we touch down, smiling blue eyes meeting smiling blue eyes. The metal beast screeches and bucks a while yet but finally slows enough to turn towards the terminal. *Home.*

I visualize family awaiting us and rebel against the long process between us, hardly containing my anticipation.

"Is this Canada?" asks Elliott reasonably but loudly as we walk the mindless customs queue, and I see heads turn and stare at the young quester. Both Stu and I look down at him, smile broadly, and nod happily at him. "Well, where is Grandma, then?"

She will be waiting for us behind a special security gate along with lots of family this time—not just Grandma.

"We have to get all our luggage first, Elliott," states our travelling sage, Jewel. "Right, Dad?"

"That's right, but first we have to prove we're safe people to enter Canada," says Stu, and I see him scoop Elliott up on his shoulders to better see the customs officials we're approaching.

Finally, giddy with weariness and chilled to the bone from tiredness, we see the family gathering awaiting us. Jewel and Elliott run to open arms while Anika frowns, lowers her head, and snuggles even lower in her stroller loaded with bags and blankets, not sure about this *Canada* place we've been talking about for so long.

I fall into hug after hug and swim in the familiar English and joking and love.

We have a whirlwind month of visiting family and as many friends as possible, and Stu is even able to coordinate a couple of interviews. We take day trips to the mountains, Elbow Falls, and Canmore; skip stones in the Bow River; picnic at Big Hill Springs Park west of Airdrie; and attend a family open house hosted at Mom and Bart's place. Foremost in my memory, a big pick-me-up for any lady, is a comment from Auntie Jolene: "You've always been such a pretty girl, Gina." At a time in life when every penny or euro is spent on essentials for our kids and home, and feeling like an old, worn-out shoe, this is the kindest thing anyone says to me.

Even the weather cooperates and gives us an unlikely warm

month for summer in the Calgary area, though the warmth of being connected to family and friends is the true blessing.

We also make time for an important day trip, Wainwright way, and visit Dad's special place. The kids help scrub the tall scripted monument, pick wildflowers to place in the vase, and dance round and round it, singing fun kids' songs in German for their Grandpa in heaven. I love their spontaneity.

As Stu helps them search the short brush edging the cemetery, looking for the knitted marker I placed there years ago, Borneo's resting place, I use the private space to repeat my promise to Dad: "I will return, Dad. I'm sorry to leave again, but I hope to visit Berlin while I'm away. I miss you so much and forever."

I feel comforted and whole for our brief time together. I walk slowly towards the parking spot, to my waiting family, treasuring my unexpected sense of peace.

November 2011

Our trip to Canada last summer, ended all too soon, and I remember my voiced angst.

"Stu, I don't want to go back to Germany. How can we leave our family and friends again, knowing the loneliness and isolation awaiting us?"

But surprisingly, I think returning was actually harder for Stu.

"Gina, I feel like I'm just stuck here. I completed my commitment here long ago. How many jobs have I applied for back in Canada? I think I've lost track. We've even tried a couple in the States. There's nothing at the universities, nothing with the government, and nothing even in the business sector. All these years of education and beaucoup dollars has got us sweet nowhere—just a fast track to major debt and poverty."

Such words from my book-smart academic surprises me. It's strange, but our roles are maybe reversing a bit. He has been strong for me for the last three years. Now maybe I need to be the strong one to get us through this adventure.

"It has been discouraging, Stu, but we'll just have to continue applying for everything that suits your CV and interests you. My promise to you is to be content in our current situation." I give a solemn salute to seal the promise.

That facetious comment definitely lightens the mood for both of us. Stu knows me well; contentment is an elusive quality despite the many blessings I enjoy. I'm always desperately seeking a secure niche to create a home nest, take root, and create beauty. I've started checking out permanent apartments to buy and settle in. Stu listens respectfully but doesn't seem to have the same motivation. He seems intent on leaving Germany behind; this is just another way we experience differing motivation.

I have actually come to love everything here except that we are so far from family and the pay scale keeps us almost destitute, as we are managing Canadian debt on German income.

What we love here, I've come to understand, is the healthy lifestyle that is almost a given and is financially sustainable simply because of the moderate climate. Things grow and are affordable. Green endures; the outdoors is inviting and accessible year-round. Transportation without owning a vehicle is manageable owing to geography and population. And our little, cocooned family-style living is a treat too—especially for Stu. I yearn for friendship connections and a wider circle, but he is content with just our home. I know his bent towards humour in relationships is a misfit for Germans. They don't get his humour at all. I'm thankful for his Romanian-French colleagues, Andrei and Sofia; they are his jovial comrades that are a good fit.

But what's ahead? Don't we all wish we knew that sometimes? Of course, it's probably best we don't know

Spring 2012

Spring is here, and I am thankful first and foremost because my laundry clothes horse can sit outside. *Will I miss my eternal interior decor of our entire apartment covered in laundry most of the week?* I ask myself, chuckling.

There are so many little things to be thankful for, and there are things to pray for too, such as a job back in Canada, an opportunity for me to visit Berlin, a decision about Elliott's eyes, Serge's struggles with MS, Langston's recovery from surgery, my grandpa's moving into assisted living and being separated from Grandma after being married seventy-two years, and so on.

I place all my concerns in God's care and, for now, refocus on an unexpected upcoming treat: Mom's recent call and offer.

"Gina, is it mid-March that Stu is taking some holiday time? I know you guys have hoped to get to Hungary sometime, and I found a timeshare in Visagrad, a couple of hours north of Budapest, right along the Danube. I'll try to book it if you guys are still interested and have the time to figure out the transportation stuff."

I wish Mom could have seen my eyes pop wide and my jaw drop a maximum drop.

"Stu will be ecstatic, Mom," I assured her. "I will text Stu and have him be certain of his holiday dates and let him get started checking on trams and buses and trains. Are you sure you want to go to Hungary, Mom?"

"Of course I am sure. You guys are the best travel guides a person could have, and I get to spend time with all of you. I'm excited already."

The last three weeks have gone as fast as a shooting star while we have been making preparations for our upcoming sprint to Hungary. The jaunt will not accommodate a stop in Berlin, so I place that longing in the back of my mind once again.

Mom has arrived, and as during each visit, my life is made so much easier with her energetic helpfulness. The kids are certainly wired, both from having Grandma here and also from knowing we'll be travelling.

"Gina, will we get all the way to the timeshare tomorrow?" Mom's question interrupts my focus on packing as much as possible into as little luggage as possible

"That is the plan. We need to get up at 0430, and after a mere fifteen hours and twenty-seven minutes, we'll hopefully arrive at the timeshare." I stare at Mom with wide-eyed audacity.

She frowns back. "How on earth will the kids manage that kind of day?"

"Stu has a family compartment booked on the ICE train parts of the trip, both directions. That will make it easier to corral the kids and give freedom to move around a bit. Are you still excited to go?" I raise my eyebrows in question.

"Sounds daunting! I think I should head to bed without supper if that is the gruelling itinerary for tomorrow" is her gutsy response, accompanied by an exaggerated yawn and shoulder rolls.

Today has been an endurance travel day, but there have been no real glitches. Our stocky Hungarian shuttle bus driver is mute on the entire trip from Budapest to the timeshare in Visagrad, likely because of the language barrier, but we arrive safely, though it is late and we are tired. Under the night's darkness, we are all disoriented and get only a cursory impression of our new place. It seems compact, tidy, and pleasingly inviting, with a substantial wooden table by the large windows overlooking the courtyard below; a wall and counter with a two-burner stove; a tiny sink and fridge; a small couch that I hope is a pull-out for Jewel and Mom to sleep on; and two tub chairs we can push together for Elliott to sleep on—our essentials all in one room!

Moving further into our place, I turn and see our bedroom. It is more spacious, showing lovely large windows, and is already set with a baby cot for Anika. The bathroom looks sparkling clean and adequate with even a tub—our preference anyway. We quickly settle in and nest.

Sunday arrives, and we discover everyone has slept well in our new digs. Elliott's two-chair bed stayed together the whole night! Everyone is hungry, and there isn't much for snacking left in the bags. We stroll uptown on quiet deserted streets in hopes of finding an open grocery store.

"Daddy, that looks like a grocery store," Jewel calls back to us from her vantage point, pointing across the street.

Fortunately, she's right, and it is open. However, recognizing anything familiar is out of the question. There are pig feet and chicken necks and scraps of indeterminate random meats that make me terrified.

"Pig feet have tasty meat on them," Mom states confidently and cheerfully. "And cream gravy over the various chicken parts will also be good. Don't worry; I'm an old farm girl from way back!"

"Thanks, Mom, but I think we'll try these packages over here. They look similar to Lipton side dishes on Canadian shelves," I say as I catch Stu's eye and subtle nod of agreement.

Some bread, cheese, veggies, and fruit complete our shopping. The only extra item is a big, colourful bulging tin that looks to be full of butter. There is a surprise when we find a can opener and open it. I think it was some type of white cheese with murky fluid all around it. Stu took a fancy to the tin and saved it for some future usage.

The lookalike side dish packages are not edible and get flushed down the toilet. I have to concede that Mom had the better idea, and I determine tomorrow we'll brave the shopping again and hire Mom as cook!

Today is a better shopping day for groceries, and Stu diverts my attention from meal planning with "Let's take this free ride up the mountain to the thirteenth-century ruins of King Matthias Corvinus of Hungary; this was his summer home, apparently. The pamphlet claims the river views of the Danube are breath-taking. Looks like we can hike our way back down after we explore the sights up there."

"Sounds good if there is room for our trusty PT cruiser stroller," I respond.

"I will find out, Gina," Stu replies. He then makes a quick call to the front desk. "We can catch a ride, stroller included," he reports afterward.

So off we go exploring, despite the bitter March cold. It has been spring-warm in Freiburg, but here we are ill prepared for the lingering winter and haven't brought warm enough clothes. Lucky Anika, snuggled in her down-filled stroller cover, fares better than the rest of us. We now understand why it was the king's summer home!

Exploring the ruins is fun, and the kids climb snow-covered rocky cliffs and sit on mammoth royal thrones, covered in snow, before we start the arduous switchback trail back down to the town. Stu and I lift the stroller over many low rock fences and gnarled roots, but the hard work helps keep us partially warm.

"I bet this is really a nice place in the summer," Mom chiming our familiar assessment and making us all laugh.

We certainly relish our eventual arrival back at our posh, warm digs of the resort.

Our suite is in a renowned Hungarian spa resort.

We splurge and enjoy a Hungarian meal in the dining room Tuesday night—what a flavourful meal!

Thursday we venture a long day back into Budapest, taking an early-morning bus. I think it is the most dramatic city we've seen so far in our European travels. We fight the icy winds as we cross the nineteenth-century chain bridge over the Danube bisecting Buda from Pest. Up castle hill there's a market square in Buda's old town, where Mom buys a fuzzy bright burgundy Cossack hat for a friend back home; she wisely made use of it to keep warm though too. She also attracts a Japanese film crew, who tug her over under the big arches, with a view of the Danube and Pest side of the city. She's probably going to be all over Japanese billboards as if representing a native Hungarian! It's amazing what a few smiles, head nods, and hand gestures can accomplish. Stu and I discreetly go the other direction, not wanting any part of the foreign filming!

There is so much to see, but every one of us, except Mom, is nearly frozen.

We are dreading the punishing headwinds we'll face once we start back across the chain bridge.

"I bet it's really nice here in the summer," Mom teases, but with no reward of laughter this time. The bridge seems endless, and it is a miracle we manage to keep all six of us together and alive. The wind mocks us, and we buffet people-traffic heading the reverse direction.

From the long day and the cold, the kids sleep on the return bus ride; thank you God.

After settling the kids into bed, I make discreet hand signals to Stu to meet me in the other room. I have a proposal to make.

"Stu, it's Mom's birthday tomorrow," I whisper conspiratorially, "and it will also be our last night here. I want to treat her. I'm thinking that after a simple supper together in our suite, I could help settle the kids for night and then take her to that lovely dining room again for a special dessert treat. Are you OK with that idea? I will bring back a Hungarian doughnut for you!" I give him a wink.

Stu pastes on a mock look of innocence. "That sounds like a good idea, Gina, and I like the sound of the Hungarian doughnut reward too, or … something chocolate."

Indeed, Friday evening finds Mom and me in the cosy and delectable privacy of the resort dining room, slowly devouring the marvellous Hungarian doughnuts and enjoying adult conversation! We remember to order a four-layer-high slice of Hungarian chocolate torte for our chocoholic sitter too.

"Mom, Torr spoke to me when she and Serge visited two years

ago about why I might be fixated on visiting Berlin." I subtly weave this into our conversation, hoping to get her insight as well.

"Really. What is her theory?" Mom asks as her hazel eyes darken and probe my blue ones. I feel a bit trapped with that penetrating look and wonder if I really want to open this can of worms.

Taking a big, quick breath for fortification, I wade in. "Well, apparently, just a couple of weeks before Dad's death, you were at work, and he and we girls had a big discussion about the recently opened Berlin Wall and the resulting new freedom for the German people after its reign of thirty devasting years." Seeing those hazel eyes still focused on me intently, I swallow, trying to moisten my dry mouth before going on. "Torr thinks the timing and connection to Dad has resulted in my unbidden fixation, despite me not remembering anything about even having the discussion." I say this quickly, looking down and piercing another small bit of dessert distractedly.

I know there is an open discussion policy in our family regarding Dad, but I still feel a need to protect Mom too and try to gauge when she is wrestling with her own grief. *Perhaps that is a piece of my hesitation to discuss this now*, I think.

"That sounds like a very astute observation. What do you think about it, Gina?" asks Mom quietly, taking a slow sip of her tea. "Have you done anything to follow up on it?"

"No. I haven't, really," I admit hesitantly, and I continue to draw little circles in my whipped cream on my plate. Then, looking back at Mom, I add, "I think about it often though. And I still want to go there."

After looking down again and studying my circle patterns on my plate in a long silence, I finally say, "I feel more reluctant since Torr told me her theory … maybe afraid somehow." My confession of fear surprises me. *What am I afraid of*, I wonder. "Doesn't make any sense, I know," I tack on lamely.

"Gina, I have a theory. It might help you. It might not. It may not relate directly to your current quandary, but I'll throw it out there anyway."

"Well, I'm open to any thoughts you have, Mom. I just don't understand my hesitancy at all."

"I've learned there are so many models of grief out there, but I favour moving *away* from the pressured goal of getting back to your *old normal.*"

We sip our tea, and I try to evaluate whether that is what I keep trying to do—become who I think I was supposed to be.

"That guideline or goal is unreasonable and unproductive," states Mom firmly as she places her teacup down gently. She reaches for my left hand on the tablecloth and says slowly, with a small smile, "You can't change the past. But it helps to admit the past changes you."

I nod and let my mind wonder about how I've changed. I always thought I'd be a lawyer, advocating for fairness and right in the world, but I suspect losing Dad influenced my priority of family over career. I know I was always an idea girl and organizer, but death in our home brought a heaping portion of sadness that tempers those skills. I was just a kid, but I was so full of confidence and positivity. That took a big hit, I know; everything became suspect and up for questioning.

I hear Mom continuing. "Would you like to hear my theory or model? I call it the Mack model."

"Because of Fort McMurray, right?" I say, smiling, feeling intrigued.

"Aren't you insightful tonight!" She says with a chuckle. "And yes, that *is* why I call it that."

I watch as she finds a pen in her slim travel purse and begins to draw on the back side of our resort reservation form, which was luckily found in there as well.

"I believe the focus has to be on knowing and accepting the new you rather than struggling to recapture the person you were before the tragedy. For me, I know I was irrevocably changed by your father's sudden death. I truly couldn't recognize *me* any more. Remember: you can't change the past, but the past does change you!"

I follow her carefully drawn lines and double figures of eight, concretely in front of me, which help me understand her words.

"So, summing up, energy and focus need to be on recognizing and accepting our changed selves and learning a new life. I was still recognizable, physically, by others, but looking outward from inside, I knew nothing remained the same."

She leans back in her chair and relaxes her shoulders and studies her folded hands on the table before looking directly at me and continuing in a soft voice. "It was a very lonely and frightening position. Perhaps similar to that of folks that have had an amputation or brain injury from a vehicle accident or a stroke, or even amnesia. Life is changed forever. So you start over and relearn who you are now rather than strive in futility to return to who you were before the loss. Does that make any sense, Gina?"

"That's a lot to take in, but I can identify with it, I think," I say, tripping over my thoughts. "So maybe it makes a lot of sense to me. I don't know; it's just a lot to think about."

"Gina, the bond you had with your dad doesn't end; you have it forever. Your heart and mind and spirit retain that bond, but recognizable, concrete aspects are gone forever."

"Yeah, no more talks and discussions and gifting and laughing and hugs and …" My throat constricts, and I can't finish my thoughts immediately. I then choke out, "Dad meeting my special Stu and my children." Quiet tears splash their way to my plate, and I reach for my cheery napkin.

We sit in silence for a while, finishing our tea, sorting through our thoughts and emotions and memories, and we then quietly pay our bill and walk arm in arm slowly down the hall and up the stairs to our suite.

A week later, back in Freiburg, I continue to mull over what Mom has shared and what my sister has told me previously, and I now feel stronger about visiting Berlin, but life's routine marches along.

I'm cycling along, enjoying the spring sun's warmth on my back. I glance behind me to check that Mom is still navigating the busy road safely. She keeps a bicycle here and also bought my workhorse bicycle just after Anika was born. *Those few months were a personal low for me*, I recall with a shiver. This bicycle I count as one of my lifesavers, right up there with my half-hour bath routine; I can't imagine my life functioning without them. Hooked up to the double-child chariot bike trailer that runs competition with the PT cruiser stroller for a family vehicle, I acknowledge today is no exception.

"Anika, are you in there, sweetie? I can only see plants and tools and bags of soil," I hear Mom say as we arrive home from the nursery and hardware stores. Silence greets us, but on closer inspection, we discover Anika has fallen asleep, slumped over a soil bag. We have enough plants and supplies to start spring gardening again and beautify the yard even more. We hope we'll get most of this done over the next couple of days, before Mom heads back to Canada. I feel lonely already thinking about her leaving, but this gently warm spring weather and the smells and promise of summer while working in our yard lift my spirit.

September 2012—Berlin

Helena, one of my German friends, is making it possible for me to finally make the trip to Berlin! It's so unexpected, but she seems to understand my fixation and need to go; she has offered to keep care of my kids for three days. I'm so excited and so nervous too, wondering what feelings this might lay bare.

Stu has a brief meeting in Stuttgart and then moves on to

Berlin, and there is room for me to tag along. I will spend the time exploring, searching, thinking, and feeling.

Stu intrudes on my reverie. "Gina, Moritz is driving tomorrow and will pick us up here at 0545. Are you all packed?"

"Yes, I am, and—"

Elliott comes running from his room, waving his prize possession, and interrupts. "Daddy, I'm packed, and I have my crank flashlight!"

"Elliott," Stu admonishes with a frown and a stern tone, "your mom and I were talking; you know not to interrupt. Now go bring your backpack and wait by the door. We will all walk over to Helena's together once everyone is ready. Can you wait patiently just a few more minutes, bud?"

Returning from Helena's, I suspect I won't be able to sleep at all tonight, but the rude alarm six hours later proves me wrong.

While driving mile after mile through the colourful fall countryside with picturesque hillside farms and small villages displaying different eras of architecture, I fall prey to its soothing charm from my window seat position. I enter in on some of the German chit-chat within the vehicle but leave most of it to others as they discuss the upcoming meetings. I'm enjoying listening to Stu in his professional role, which is so different from his family role. I feel like a spy or intruder and stifle a chuckle. My mind flashes to my dad's work world in Saskatchewan when I was just a kid and got to visit his workspace; I remember writing all over the big whiteboard at his office, spinning round and round in his big, high-backed office chair, and heating treats in the microwave there. Both of his secretaries seemed such fancy ladies, I thought, and were always friendly to me, the Boss's youngest rug rat. I don't remember visiting his three sites in the Fort Mack area. My mind goes blank—just a flash of all the company people at the funeral … faces of strangers.

"Gina, wake up sleepyhead." Stu nudges me and whispers in my ear, "We're here." It's almost midnight, and we all scatter to our rooms, hoping to be rested for tomorrow.

As Stu heads out early to a breakfast meeting, he says, "I left a room key for you on the dresser. Call me if you get lost." He then turns back, bends his head to my ear, and whispers, "Jo-Gina Rayida," using my dad's pet name for me. I smile as our eyes lock, and I feel understood in my quest for connecting to Dad.

I head out a little later, psyched for a day of exploring; I'm alert, wary, and exhilarated. I return to our main-floor hotel room just as the sun is setting. My feet are sore from all my walking, and I'm as thirsty as a camel as I navigate the bright hotel reception area and head to our room hoping I don't run into anyone I know. I want to hold my thoughts and feelings to myself.

I reach my door, turn the ornate key in the lock, and gaze at the fresh space. It is small and European-sparse, but the crisp white linens are elegantly showcased against navy foot throws and full-length drapery framing a patio door to the subtle lighting of the park-like outdoors. As I scan the room, I notice a little note on my pillow. "Gone for the evening meal with the gang, but not likely very late. Call me when you get in, signed, Your Stu." Below is his endearing, ever-present drawing of Smoker the Dog.

This brings a fond smile, but I realize, *I'm glad to be alone, actually; I can try to sort out my thoughts and feelings.* After I call Stu, I'm going to just soak away my jumbled thoughts, lie in the deep tub, and sip on ice water.

Amidst the lavender-scented bubbles, I start to wonder how the kids are managing at Helena's busy home, but I feel myself dozing off.

I'm ten years old and upstairs in N. C.'s bedroom in Fort McMurray, arguing about who gets shotgun position next time we're in the car, when I hear the front door open, signalling Dad is home. Giving a withering look to N. C., I turn and tear down the stairway; I have an important question for Dad. The stairs turn into an up escalator, and I struggle and struggle to get to the bottom while my frustration rises. At last I get to the bottom and shout out, "Dad, I have a question for you!"

"What is it, Jo-Gina Rayida?" I hear him call back from the kitchen. Again I struggle to make the short stretch of hallway to the kitchen, where I can hear him and Mom talking and laughing. The hallway just never ends, no matter how many steps I manage, but I can see them, backs to me, as Mom is preparing supper. The kitchen is my small, familiar, walk-through galley kitchen in Freiburg. I'm my adult self now, married with children, and still my voice won't work. Over and over I try to call out my important question, but I can't voice it. I can see Dad clearly now, in his navy dress pants and brown tweed sports jacket, back from Calgary or Edmonton meetings. Borneo's black nose and green eyes are peeking out at me from the crook of Dad's arm, and just as Dad begins turning towards me, revealing his clean-cut short sideburns, one side of his widow's peak with a little wave, and just a glimpse of his neat moustache, he starts to lift a pot lid to check out its tantalizing aromas. The lid slips out of his hand, and a frightened Borneo leaps out of his arms and races towards me before the lid even hits the floor. With the crash, I wake up in frustration and surprise, and I realize my phone is ringing in the bedroom and has interrupted my dream.

My bath has cooled, and I'm feeling discouraged, having missed my opportunity to talk with Dad and ask my important question. In my anger, I dry off vigorously and then find my phone. Seeing the call is not a number I recognize, I throw it down again in futility.

Knowing Stu will be back soon, I simply crawl into bed and snuggle under the down duvet.

"How was your day of exploration, Gina?" Stu asks as he enters, hangs his suit jacket carefully on the back of a chair, and saunters over to me in my bed linens' swaddle.

Sitting on the bed with one leg crooked casually over the edge, he listens intently to my day, starting with my recounting of the dream.

"So what was your important question for your dad?" he asks, cocking his head a bit and looking intently at me, face pinched in anticipation.

"I don't know, Stu," I say in exasperation, sitting up quickly, throwing back some of the weight of the duvet, and pressing my fists into the mattress as my eyes dart furiously around the room. "That's the frustrating part!"

Breathless now, I say more calmly, "That's dreams for you, I guess," as Stu solemnly reaches for both my hands. "At least I got to see him. Vividly. Hear his voice, smell the scent of his aftershave. Hear him call me his pet name. You called me that this morning too." I turn to face him directly. "Remember?" Without waiting for an answer, I forge ahead. "I think, just being here in Berlin, I feel understood in my grief and loss, my story of separation. I feel a connection to my dad, knowing he visited this area at about my same age and likely felt some of my same emotions—especially as the wall was still intact at that time. Maybe this dream shows me that too—an adult connectedness, not just a child–dad connectedness. Do you think a dead person can visit us here on Earth, Stu?" I wonder whether he'll think I'm crazy or overreacting.

Still holding my hands and rubbing them gently, he replies, "I think you certainly had an important visit this evening. I'm happy for you, Gina; you're getting some pieces of memory of your dad back." After a thoughtful silence, he changes the subject, saying nonchalantly, "Oh, by the way, I have a surprise for you."

I glance around the room for any evidence, and I then notice a take-out box up on the clothes rack shelf and slowly get out of bed. *Could it be?*

Stu reaches above me, fetches the box down, and proudly presents it with both hands.

Opening it up carefully, I shake my head at his thoughtfulness; press my lips together, containing my spreading smile of delight; and take a deep, pleasureful breath. There lies a healthy slice of *apfelkuchen* and a sealed container of accompanying *vanillesosse*.

I willingly share my special treat, and between small, savoured bites, I relay the rest of my day's exploration.

Climbing back under the covers to quell my shaking that always accompanies strong emotion, I admit, "You know, despite my plan to guard my heart, I found it pretty overwhelming today."

Twisting my sapphire ring round and round on my slim finger, I look down, and my mind flashes back to Macklin days and the excitement of receiving such a beautiful and costly gift, a present from my parents on their trip to Thailand to visit Dad's sister, who was volunteering in a refugee camp as a nurse.

I clasp my hands together to stop my nervous twisting and continue. "I suspect I experienced every emotion known to humans, Stu. I know I felt huge sadness and grief—not just my own, but that represented through the cold war—as I visited the many historic sites. Also, I felt surprise, anger, and disgust. I even experienced admiration and a growing hope and trust in humanity as I ate up and digested the unexpected freedom victory of November 1989, when the destruction of the wall began."

"Like the reminder of your family discussion back then that Victoria shared with you," Stu interjected.

"Exactly," I say, nodding vigorously. "But I also experienced a niggling, smouldering fear that we humans are prone to repeat our mistakes!" A shiver overtakes me, and I say, "I'm looking forward to getting back home to the kids." *Back to our snug-as-a-bug-in-a-rug little nest*, I think as we turn in for the night.

December 2012

Our little family Christmas is so cosy and meaningful. We always miss the larger family times we'd be having in Canada, but these times of just us have become precious to us. Germany has been surprising in many ways, and the overt Christian influence has been one of the surprises.

The state school our children attend even has religion classes. One year the class is taught by Protestants, and the next year by the Catholics. I well recall Jewel's question a couple of years back: "Mom, are we Catholic or Protestant?"

I wondered what brought that question forward and tried to decipher what was behind the question before I gave a simple answer.

"That's an interesting question with really big words and ideas, my sweet treat. What did you want to know about it?" I asked as I sat down on a stool in front her and peered into the big, blue see-all eyes of my firstborn.

"Well, you know how much I like religion class and that I love Frau Klein. She always makes the Bible stories so real and fun, and we kids act out the stories and make recipes and eat olden-days food, and she always listens to our questions, and I know she loves God so much and she loves us too." Running out of breath, Jewel stopped suddenly, and she then continued. "Frau Klein is Catholic, and I want to go to her church. Frau Hahn is Protestant, and she isn't any fun and just reads a story and has us colour something while she is busy doing something else. I don't think she is interested in us or God," proclaimed my wise sage of only seven years. She had discerned true religion.

Now how do I break it to her that we aren't Catholic?

"You always have such good questions Jewel. And you have such wisdom. You have discerned which of your leaders really cares and shows love and is excited about God. I truly think that God doesn't care one wit about which church we worship in, but rather what is in our hearts and how we treat others. The church we attend is not Catholic, but you have fun Sunday school teachers there, right? I'm glad you enjoy Frau Klein so much, and maybe we can attend her church sometime too, especially if it is the one right here in Rieselfeld. Just ask her, and I'm sure she will let you know. We chose the church we attend because it has English and German in each service, but now we all have fairly good German language skills— especially you, my little linguist." I hug her close. "Would you like to make a special gift for Frau Klein, to thank her for the fun class she creates each week?" I ask, knowing how much she loves to make things and likes giving to others.

Face alight, she shares her ready ideas. "Oh, could we make one of those cloth bags like we made at my last birthday party? I know Frau Klein likes purple."

There have been many such questions about faith and differing religious practices over the years, and as a parent I have appreciated the presence of God-awareness in the state school here. All special Christian observances like Christmas and Easter are fully celebrated. That has been lost in Canada under the guise of multiculturalism.

This Christmas the kids again want to do something special for the many homeless people they see every time we are downtown. Elliot has such a heart for them and can't find a place in his brain to understand how a person could not have a family, or a home to go to. Without words to convey it, I think he is realizing he is a fortunate soul to have his family and a safe home, despite how irritating it is to have sisters in his way!

"Mom, can I count the five euros into each goodie bag?" asks Elliott, holding up and frantically jingling the jar of precious euros saved over the last few months, his blonde curls jiggling as well. I nod, enjoying the bright shine of his excited blue eyes, as Jewel chimes in, "I'm putting the choco lebkuchen in."

"Anika, here are the oranges and chocolates for you to put in each bag," I say, and I bend down to catch her running from their play table. "Oops, let's get these washed up first," I say, and I give a love squeeze to sticky little hands.

"I want to do the buying of the fresh butter pretzels at the Backerei," states Elliott, glancing up at me hopefully.

"You can buy half and Jewel can buy half," I reply in fairness. His stormy face looks back at me, but he nods in defeat, and we head to the tram for our annual outing.

As we get off near the plaza, where the homeless people hang about, Anika chooses to stay safely in her stroller and Jewel clings to me. Elliott fearlessly grabs the gift bags we've made and runs over to each one and gives a bag; he goes back and forth till all have one.

"Mom, do we have one more bag? There's a new lady over there, and she looks cold and hungry too," he pleads as he points.

"Sorry, my boy. That was the last bag. But we can put another together tonight and bring it tomorrow. Go tell her that, if you like."

With relief showing on his face, he thanks me, and with full energy, he races back to the lady with his youthful promise.

My own cares and concerns about dirt and lice and disease shrink in the face of seeing my son's excitement and their faces of joy, which are smiling as much from being around the children as getting the gifts, I suspect. *What memories are stirred for these people?* I wonder. Over the years, we've come to feel connected to some of them. Most Sundays, we see Dieter, who told me clearly during our first meeting, when Stu and I offered to buy him a coffee, "Yes, please, and I want six sugars and lots of cream." I will never forget him.

In many ways, I guess I've experienced a similar situation of displacement, being a faceless immigrant, not really fitting in to the place around me but appreciating the bits of kindness shown by a few understanding fellow beings. And as on every Christmas, I acknowledge my orphan state, missing Dad acutely. As Elliott races back towards me, I wonder again about the stories of loss within each of these beleaguered souls.

Returning the next day, Elliott finds the new lady and presents her with the promised goodie bag of love. Dieter even has a candy for each of the kids, giving back what he can.

Back in our own home, I drink in the contrasting warmth of our snug little domain. I like to fill our apartment with the sounds, smells, and look of Christmas. Stu is just as bad, so it is very Christmassy around here! We've added special German baking to our traditions now too. I particularly like making *lebkuchen keks* and *hildebrotchen*. I promised Mom I'd save a few for her.

I know she is bringing a box of Sunny Boy hot cereal with her when she arrives at the end of the month. We'll make the trade then! The kids are so excited about it. Last year Mom mailed us a box, and it cost $98. It was the best gift that Christmas. The kids get tired of oatmeal for every breakfast despite Stu's many concoctions.

My closest German friend, Helena, saw what it cost to have it shipped from Canada and was horrified. She said she could help me find the ingredients here and make it. She's been an angel in human form to me and has guided me respectfully in the many subtle but essential German ways. I know I still have a lot to learn, linguistically and culturally, but Helena has softened the blow.

Jewel breaks into my reverie. "Mom, when does Grandma get here? Tomorrow on the train?"

"That's right," I answer, and I literally shake myself to come back to the present. "Shall we go down to the *hauptbahnhof* to meet her? You know sometimes her flight to Frankfurt is a bit too late for her to catch the early train; we can't be sure which train she will be on," I remind her.

"I'm praying she'll be on the earliest one. Let's go please, please, Mom." Elliott and Anika get in on the sing-song begging pleas.

"Sounds like a plan, but promise—no tears or complaining if she isn't on that train and we have to come home without her," I bargain.

"We promise!" all three chorus loudly and with expectant faces, jumping up and down in anticipation of having a house guest again.

"Guys," Stu inserts, "You know the only reason Grandma is coming is to experience the New Year's tradition of fireworks."

"No, Dad, she is coming to deliver the box of Sunny Boy so we don't have to eat oatmeal tomorrow," Jewel teases right back with hands on her hips and her chin at a saucy angle.

"Grr! I'll show you who has to eat oatmeal!" shouts Stu, and he starts the screaming chase around the house. *Good thing we have no one living beneath our suite*, I think for the millionth time.

The next day, as the train begins to slow, we watch the passing exit door windows expectantly for signs of Mom, and I pray for the sake of the kids that she managed to catch the first ICE out of Frankfurt.

"I see her, I see her!" Elliott shouts, and he pulls me urgently through the clot of people.

"Thank you, God," I whisper as we descend on Mom with glee and hugs and a million questions. I stand apart a bit and find myself studying her more closely as the kids swarm her. She looks so tired. Is she ageing? Do I see more grey strands escaping her jaunty wool beret? How many more years will she manage the long flight and time change? *I need you, Mom; don't ever get old*, I admonish, facetiously, in silence.

"Did you remember to bring Sunny Boy, Grandma?" Elliot asks while pulling on her French-styled multicoloured coat sleeve and rubbing his fingers on the fine corduroy.

"I brought two boxes, Elliot! That's why this suitcase is so heavy. Can you pull it for me, my strong boy?" she responds.

"Did you have a fun Christmas, Grandma?" asks Jewel, reaching for Grandma's other hand.

"I sure did, and I've brought matching pyjama loungers for Elliott and your dad in my suitcase. This is the year for the guys, so they all get a pair, in Canada and here in Germany too."

"Grandma, are you excited to spend New Year's Eve with us and watch our fireworks?" probes Elliott while he slants a look at his dad.

"I certainly am, and you can demonstrate your prowess in lighting a few, right?" she challenges in a cheery voice, looking down into his proud face.

"We've bought a whole bunch, Grandma: ground spinners and sparklers, fountains, and Roman candles. Are you going to try lighting one?" He looks up at Grandma with eyes ablaze with wonder.

"Of course I'll light one, Elliott. Thanks for sharing the fun."

I'm thinking this could prove very interesting indeed—my mom lighting scary fireworks. *This I want to see*, I think with a hidden smile.

Finally, safely away from the milling crowd on the main platform, Mom crouches down to greet our almost two-year-old Anika, who is cocooned in her down-filled stroller sleeping bag. Yes, in just five days she'll be two—our Germany-born daughter. How the time has flown by.

"So how are you, my German dolly?" I hear Mom ask. Big blue eyes smile back, and I see Anika poke one mittened hand out in greeting.

"Lub you, Gramma" is her enthusiastic response.

Tram number five's arrival ends our conversations. Throngs of people clamour to get on while we all scan for the right door to accommodate the stroller.

Right now, it's midnight in Canada, and I know Mom is struggling to stay awake. She doesn't handle the eight-hour time change well. I recall one time on her return to Canada, while Bart was away flying, she put eggs on to boil and fell sound asleep in the living room. Auntie Lauren happened to call and woke her, but the house was full of smoke and Mom was disoriented. We all believe Auntie Lauren saved her life. The stove was another matter. Apparently their glass cook top now has a permanent divot as a memento.

"Grandma, is this the day our grandpa in heaven died?" blurts Elliott as we all exit the tram and start walking to our apartment block.

Now that should rouse Mom from her sluggishness, I think uneasily. My kids know this is a day I find difficult—a death anniversary. We should have stopped at the Minster on the way home from the Hauptbahnhof and lit a candle in memory, as we usually do; I know Mom would have liked that too.

"Elliott, it certainly is," Mom manages to say. "Thanks for remembering. Maybe when we light firecrackers on New Year's Eve, we can dedicate one to Grandpa in heaven."

"Yeah, let's do that, Grandma!" he says enthusiastically as he continues running circles around her. "Dad, when we get home, can I go choose which one we'll light to honour Grandpa in heaven?"

"You just choose one in your mind, Bud. I don't like playing around with them indoors. We can save the one you choose for our final light that night. How will that be?"

"I guess" is his disappointed response as we enter the apartment and he runs off excitedly to show Grandma his Christmas haul.

As Mom settles into the kids' bedroom, knowing she will be sharing the bottom bunk with little Anika, I warn her, "Mom, I suspect that, come morning, all three will be tangled in with you!"

"Well, that's great. It will keep me warm." She winks, acknowledging our frugal heating regime.

We are all looking forward to welcoming in the new year again, especially with Mom to join in.

New Year's Eve here in Freiburg, and I suspect all over Germany, is a sight to behold. By midnight the air is thick with smoke, and we can't see across our yard to the spielplatz. But the beauty of colour throughout the evening, up till the smoke occludes everything, is exciting and unimaginable. More and more, I am coming to feel at home here. I know I need to be settled one way or another. I can't deal with continuing to put down roots here if we stay focused on returning to Canada. Something has to give. I'm at a crossroads for sure. I know which direction Stu is leaning towards.

December 2013

I still can't believe it.

I am back living in Canada, my home and native land! It's been four months already. We simply took the plunge last summer. The crossroads loomed bigger and bigger, and we had to decide. We could see our kids were becoming fully entrenched in German culture, and all of us were forging relationships, putting down roots that would be harder and harder to uproot. We needed to choose Germany or choose Canada and eliminate the dual pull; it was now or never. Stu's strong vote for Canada tipped the scale and gave the courage for our free fall. No job. No university with funds for a researcher.

We chose Edmonton, knowing the University of Alberta was where Stu wanted to continue his research. He has found an interim job in the business sector for now, and he keeps alert to openings back in his field of science.

The kids are in a school that teaches in German in the mornings and English in the afternoon. Of course, Anika gets to stay home with me, which she loves. In Germany, she had already started school as a three-year-old; some kids started even earlier. The teachers loved having her because she spoke German fairly well and she was even potty-trained. Lots of parents left that job for the school to do!

Being back in Canada, we've had lots of family gatherings, and life seems so simple when you know the culture and the language. I know how to explain homework questions to the kids and speak maturely to their teachers. I can totally understand a sermon while sitting in a church service. I can pursue friendship confidently. I have a fully workable kitchen again and a comfortable mattress to sleep on. The bathroom door can be locked because there is the luxury of an extra half bath. I even have an electric clothes dryer again!

So why am I feeling sad and grieving for my dad? Perhaps, as Mom suggests, this grief is a constant partner in life—a partner to get to know, not avoid or run from.

I know that having been only eleven years old, I was totally unprepared to deal with my dad's sudden death. I hadn't known I needed to pay attention to everything about him so I would be able to hold on and savour the memories if he were suddenly snatched away. I hadn't known a parent could just vanish in a single moment.

I hadn't known how much I needed him. I didn't realize I would resent friends who still had their dads and didn't appreciate them. I didn't realize I would struggle with trust that God would care for me and my family—an awareness that any horrible thing that could happen could happen to me.

There is no immunity; it's not an option. Some might say I had to grow up a bit too soon. Adulthood seems to be about acceptance of these realities.

I made my promised return visit to his gravesite, all alone this time in September, while the kids were in school and Anika was visiting with Grandma.

I poured my heart out.

"Dad, I've done the best I could through the years," I say solemnly, in the stillness of the country cemetery. I feel the sun's warmth on my fair skin and allow the soft breeze to lift my hair lightly.

"I hope you are proud of me and my decisions—choosing marriage and family life, and facing all of life's challenges head on."

I wait in silence.

Hearing no answer, I continue.

"But now, back here in Canada, I feel I've come full circle. My heart, mind, and soul cry out for space to look at my pain of losing you.

I miss you, Dad. I just miss you."

Quiet roars in my ears, and suddenly I remember my interrupted dream in Berlin. Standing up straighter, I suddenly have an inspiration.

"I think I remember the important question I have for you!"

After a pause and clearing my throat, I throw my hands skyward, and turning a full circle, I ask clearly, "Can you see me? If I could just be certain that you still see me—me and Stu and our kids, your grandkids—I think I would be content."

I hear some crows squabbling overhead and the gentle fall breeze rustling leaves in the nearby bushes. I lay my light jean jacket down over the grave and feel the warmth of the ground beneath me as I lie down and gaze up at the soft clouds floating above me in the blue sky. My breathing slows, my body relaxes, and I inhale the fall smell of ripe highbush cranberries. I feel at peace. I feel loved. I feel whole.

Driving Highway 16 the two hours back to Edmonton, my thoughts stay focused on Dad. I wish I could remember more about him and more about our family when we were still all together. Mom believes his eleven years of loving presence in my life are deep and firm in my subconscious and give me strength; this is still a precious gift to me.

My mind wanders to what I do remember. Dad believed in a pecking order and sometimes scolded me for getting ahead of myself or my siblings.

"Gina," he'd say, dipping his head down and to the right a tad. He'd give his moustache a lick as if to be sure it was still there, raise his eyebrows, and rest his hands lightly on my shoulders, and he'd then continue. "You, young lady, need to step back. Wait your turn. You are the youngest. Don't be so pushy!" It seems he was often reminding me that everything has its own time and shouldn't be rushed. I was the youngest and needed to learn to wait and honour the pecking order.

He learned that pecking order growing up on his family farm. He had so many funny stories of his young farming life as a child.

I think visiting the gravesite, just a mile from that family farm, ignited a memory of his stories. As the fifth in the family of seven kids, he knew he had to bend to the wishes of the older four.

He spoke of his older siblings ganging up on him and throwing him in the turkey pen for the old gobbler to chase and attack him— sibling punishment meted out for order and control. It was not a "bubble wrap" society back then! I haven't learned the waiting-my-turn or patience-is-a-virtue lessons yet, I'm afraid.

Are you chuckling, Dad? I ask silently.

Now Christmastime is near, and I have a great story of my own.

Our first camping trip back in Canada last summer, in beautiful British Columbia, brought someone new into my life—Niles. The kids spotted this scrawny, skittery kitten, just weeks old and very wild. Bit by bit, with saucers of milk and tentative, gentle petting, trust grew.

Our perseverance was rewarded, and we secured him in our large cooler and put sand from the lake in a basin as a travelling litter box. We stopped in Sparwood for a proper travel cage Stu found on Kijiji.

Looking at Stu, I said, "You know we are crazy, right? Elliott is so allergic. How will this work out when he gets home from Grandma's place?"

"Let's just see what happens," he said, not looking too hopeful.

Our strategy was to keep Niles in the garage for nights, outdoors for potty times, and in our home for short spells during the day, bit by bit extending those times. Elliott still reacted, and we knew we had to find Niles another home unless Elliott could discipline himself to not touch Niles but just use the stick toy and toss toys, run outside with him, and so on.

As winter set in, Niles needed to be inside more. Miraculously, Elliott grew to tolerate Niles and play with him more and more.

Now, while Christmas approaches and my heart's memory reopens my loss of Dad, I allow Niles to be my Borneo replacement, and I weep daily whenever home alone. Niles absorbs my pain. Heart hardness that has crept in melts away in his care and understanding. I thank God for giving me this gift and taking Elliott's allergy away so I could have Niles in my life.

"Wherever you are, Dad, I hope you can see all your wonderful, talented, and quirky grandkids, and that you are proud of them and us. All of them want to meet you, and bit by bit they are learning how to miss you and yet love Grandpa Bart. You are their grandpa in heaven—a distinguished title. I hope you like it."

EPILOGUE

Summer 2014

I hear the shower running and realize Bart is already awake. I peek at the clock and see it's still really early, but the summer sun is flooding the room anyway. Neither of us have work for the next five days, and we relish having no alarms on such days!

Still, I'm glad we've woken early to get a good start on a leisurely drive to our Fairmont condo for a few days with kids and grandkids.

Feeling lazy, I take time to feast my eyes on our cheery room, with its soft yellow walls, French white furniture, and yellow-and-white striped drapery panels, all accented by a cornice and bedding in red and yellow quilting; I feel so at home.

But, like many a time before, what feeds my heart and life again is the visual gift of family surrounding me, portrayed in the many white-framed photos. I marvel at the uniqueness of each one looking back at me and commit them to God's love and care anew.

Love is painful.

I feel my heart contract as I think of the challenges they each face. I want to protect them, but I know the twists and turns in life are what shape us, often changing our strengths, gifts, and sometimes even our calling. It can result in heart hardening, but sometimes it creates sensitivity, if we allow that.

But beware. The sensitive heart is vulnerable to the painful side of love.

After getting ready for the day and the frantic loading of the car, always knowing we'll forget something, we set out west, not stopping till past Cochrane, and follow Highway 2A to Grotto Pond.

We find a parking spot, and Bart immediately heads to the water's edge with his fly-fishing gear. I place the picnic basket on the bold, colourful picnic cloth I've spread on the sturdy table, and I then carefully pick my way down the shady, root-hazard-laden bank to join Bart at the narrow, spongy shore.

Fishing is an experience in quiet, I think, and despite all the visible fishermen I can see around the shoreline, on the boardwalk to the south, and out in the water, the only sound to greet me is the soft lapping of timid waves.

I touch Bart on his shoulder to signal I'm heading out on the trail around the pond, and I leave a granola bar atop his tackle box. Today I hope to do the complete perimeter. The woodsy path and tall grasses bordering it envelop me in welcome.

After a while, the path takes a turn up a steeper section before heading into the forest. I take the steep section at a run and stop to catch my breath where it plateaus, bent over with my hands on my knees. *I guess I'm not as fit as I used to be*, I laugh inwardly.

Looking back to where I can still see a miniature version of Bart, I wave and think I see his return wave.

I pause to survey the quiet panoramic view before me of water, mountain, forest, and sky. I breathe it in deeply, acknowledging my need for solitude; it is as primal as air, water, and music for me.

Feeling my heart still pounding from the climb, my mind plays images of similar days—days of camping and hiking with Quinn when our family was still whole, before my heart exploded into a million pieces.

I never even got to say goodbye.

That shattered heart I later entrusted to our long-time friend.

But I realize now that his fear of love and constant shadow of guilt led him to abandon and reject me and my daughters—again with no goodbye.

My heart remains a heart of sorrow, acquainted with grief, and with glimpses of latent, muzzled anger at times as well.

Yet, against all odds, my heart still beats.

It beats in gratitude to God for life itself.

It beats gently for friends and family.

It beats cautiously for Bart and his family.

It beats strong and steady for my girls and their chosen mates.

It beats expressively for all my grandchildren, my complex legacy of living.

I sit down in the grass in my private contemplative space, with the warmth of the sun balancing the chill of my emotions. I pick up a small handful of soft earth to let it run through my fingers like time. As I close my eyes and wonder if I've even fallen asleep, a soft wind disturbs a few wisps of hair across my face, bringing me back to my task at hand.

I jump up awkwardly and look up the trail, deciding whether I should even take time to complete the circle now. As I gaze up the trail, my breath catches in surprise and caution yet incredible delight. A big black bear lumbers across the path and disappears into the thick forest like magic. She doesn't even bother to look my way! Then, immediately, her two frolicking cubs follow her and disappear in similar fashion. I'm captivated with the thrill and honour of glimpsing up close one of God's wild creatures, while simultaneously acknowledging my good fortune of mere moments—a tentative safety zone. I smile in edgy delight but wisely turn and head back to even safer ground!

After ravenously sharing our picnic lunch and our stories, including that of another "no catch" day for my fisherman, Bart and I head on to Canmore. We pick up our traditional maple bagels to accompany us through the mountain drive with its delicious aroma.

Our next stop should be in beautiful British Columbia and the ice cream shop in Radium, but today we choose an unexpected delay. Taking Highway 93, we stop not long after the Vermillion Crossing, shocked and surprised. We had prepared our minds for dramatic bareness, which we expected following the widespread wildfires of previous summers. The beautiful stately forests of evergreens indeed are gone, and we acknowledge a haunting, sooty blackness. But it simply serves to create a dramatic background for the all-encompassing forefront—a wash of spectacular purple.

Standing on the shoulder of the road with Bart's arm around my waist and holiday traffic whizzing by, I snap off a series of photos to capture the beauty and the memory.

Fireweed!

Beauty from ashes!

I know it immediately from my childhood.

Growing up on a small Albertan farm, I had admired this same bounteous beauty on the partly torched brush piles created by my dad as he was clearing land for future grain fields. Now I realize the message of hope and regeneration that this fireweed sings out loudly for all to hear. Last summer's devastation is now replaced with hearty, resplendent beauty to encourage one and all.

In my heart, I feel I understand the meaning of "beauty from ashes", which is reflected in my own life's journey. These little glimpses keep music singing in my own soul. May there always be enough glimpses.

CPSIA information can be obtained
at www.ICGtesting.com
Printed in the USA
BVHW071142110820
585990BV00001B/1

9 781663 204776